Stirred
BUT NOT
SHAKEN

Stirred
BUT NOT
SHAKEN

DEEP SHIVA

Srishti
PUBLISHERS & DISTRIBUTORS

SRISHTI PUBLISHERS & DISTRIBUTORS
Registered Office: N-16, C.R. Park
New Delhi – 110 019
Corporate Office: 212A, Peacock Lane
Shahpur Jat, New Delhi – 110 049
editorial@srishtipublishers.com

First published by
Srishti Publishers & Distributors in 2017

To Mom and Dad
&
The ladies in my life –
My dear daughter and lovely wife.

When you reach for the stars you may not quite get one, but you won't come up with a handful of mud either.

– Leo Burnett

Acknowledgements

I salute my parents for instilling the habit of reading in me.

I don't know precisely what inspired me to write, maybe all those comics that I had read during summer vacations or those thick books that transported me to imaginary worlds and fuelled my imagination over the years.

It only takes a moment to happen when something has to. I came home with a pc note book one fine day, stared at the blank screen, conjuring words, spinning tales in my mind and then that moment arrived when I punched the first words and kept going.

My heartfelt gratitude to all my friends and colleagues who believed in me, especially Irmeen Farhat Ali, who painstakingly went through the script and gave her frank opinion on the same. Thanks a lot girl.

To Viren Janee, for instilling confidence in me; to Marshal Chakraborty and Puneet Singh for playing their part in the whole process. Thanks a lot guys.

To Srishti Publishers for encouraging first timers like me.

And to you, my dear reader, for having picked up this book. I hope you will enjoy reading every bit of it as much as I loved writing it.

The Sheep, the Owl
and the Mouse

(I)

"Monu, if you fail in the final result na, we promise, we will put you in a government school," Mom exclaimed in an anxious tone while riding on our Priya scooter with me and Dad. The three of us were on our way to my school.

This was not new to me. Year on year, Mom and Dad would pray to god that their son did not fail.

The ten-minute ride to my school would always be in profound tension. My parents had this sad, morbid expression on their faces all the way, as if it was *their* result at stake, not mine.

"Do you even understand how much pain we take for your education in such an expensive school? Mohit, wake up!" Suddenly, Mom started to shake me, yelling on a shrill pitch, "Wake up Mohit... Wake up! It's time."

I half opened my eyes and realized that I was at Sameer's bachelor pad in Delhi. He was shaking me furiously. "Wake up, you fool!"

I was fully awake by now, what with all the shaking and shrieking. He stood in front of me with a boiled egg in one hand, a comb in the other and a towel wrapped around his waist. He shoved the full boiled egg in his mouth hurriedly, simultaneously trying to rub me with profanities.

"You certainly are an ass. It's been three months that you have been trying to find a job, and now, when you've got the first opportunity, the first interview, sahib is sleeping."

I lazily sat up, trying to understand what my dear friend was saying with his mouth full of egg. The only thing that I managed to concentrate on was his mouth; the egg was now reduced to a paste and he was rolling it in his mouth, chomping noisily.

I dragged myself out of the cot and it creaked in protest. I rubbed my eyes as Sameer poked his finger at me. "The interview is at 9, and it's already 7.30. Wake up, CEO sahib! Your *janta* is waiting," he said sarcastically. I nodded in response, just to make him stop shouting so early in the morning, but he continued nonetheless. "And one more thing, don't forget to bring an extra pair of pencil cells, the ones in the clock are now as hopeless and lazy as you are."

"Now listen," I said yawning. "Don't be overdramatic."

Shaking his head, flashing an ugly smile with his teeth still smeared with remains of the egg, he tucked his shirt into the trousers, zipped up and left in a hurry.

I grabbed my towel from the balcony and ambled across the hall to the bathroom. There was no time to laze around in the flat with a cup of tea in my hand, which had been my daily routine for the last few months. Not today, not now.

I came out fifteen minutes later, passably not pleasurably fresh because it would have taken another half an hour to do that.

"No time for a leisurely breakfast," I murmured under my breath, buttoning up the shirt.

Ten more minutes were spent in zipping up the trousers, a quick adjustment of the tie, slipping into the shoes and grabbing hold of the folder containing my credentials. It's only when you are pressing for time that you notice how long these small chores take. I grabbed my share of boiled eggs from the kitchen and dashed for the door.

In another fifteen minutes, I was in an auto, heading towards Okhla from Patparganj.

I checked my watch hoping against hope that the dreadful early morning traffic in Delhi would be thin.

Wishful thinking! I knew I was late and also knew that this job interview was very important for me.

I would not have imagined zooming across Delhi three months ago, had there not been a chance encounter with Sameer in the bazaar of Sirsaganj – a small sleepy town in the heart of Uttar Pradesh – my hometown.

It all happened one fine day, when I was strolling through the Vikas Baazar in Sirsaganj. I was lost in thought, mentally preparing and rehearsing the sales pitch for clients I had to meet. With three prospects in mind, I was mentally rehearsing three separate stories to convince them on taking a policy that day.

I was an insurance agent. A dedicated one for sure, I kept my eyes and ears open, smiled and said hello to every distantly familiar uncle and aunty, asked Mrs Sharma about their neighbour Tiwari ji, discussed politics with Verma ji, gave tuitions to Mr Madaan's daughter, played cricket with Mirza Sarfaraj's son – all this in a day, just to get some sales leads from them.

It seemed easy and it seemed fun. Like, even if you don't agree with Mr Verma on his political views, you still praise him for his farsightedness.

So, completely engrossed in those thoughts, I walked on autopilot that day. That's when, suddenly, somebody bumped into me.

I lost my balance and barely managed to save myself from falling, the bag on my shoulder slipped to the ground.

"*Teri!*" I shouted out loud, but had to abort a slew of profanities that I was about to deliver, because in front of me was Sameer with his trademark lopsided grin, wearing a suede jacket and a pair of Levi's.

"Hey, hey! Buddy cool, no *gaalis,*" he said as he shouldered me with his arms, embracing me with affection.

We had met after long and when the conversation began to flow, I asked him to come home with me. As we sat comfortably on the sofa, he reasoned with me, "Come over to Delhi! You would get better job prospects there, more suitable to your calibre. Then why waste time in this small city?"

Sameer was my buddy and classmate since kindergarten, but he had later moved to Bangalore for further studies, did his engineering, and a post-graduation in management soon followed.

On the other hand, I continued studying in Sirsaganj. It wasn't as if I had no interest in studying in a bigger town with better facilities, but I had my own situations to deal with. First, I was a mediocre student, thus merit and scholarships in good colleges of the country was out of question.

Second, I come from a humble background, my father being a clerk in a local cooperative society, so donations were also out of question.

Making me study in the *only* English medium school in the town was the biggest achievement of my parents.

They wanted to give me the best of schooling while managing with whatever little earnings they had.

I lingered on, class after class, and finally they heaved a sigh of relief when I passed the final board examination.

Sameer, on the other hand, came from a very different background; his father had a brick factory and vast farmlands. He belonged to the upper rich strata of our town and most importantly, he was also a top scorer throughout school. Still, we were the best of friends.

"See, you are wasting precious time in this town. It is time to build your career in a big city," Sameer said chewing on some homemade *mathries*. "I am not saying that you would find a suitable job immediately, but till then, you can continue with your insurance business in Delhi too."

(II)

"Saab, cooper mill compound *aagaya*." The autowalla broke my reverie as I reached Okhla.

I looked at my watch and noticed that I was already half an hour late for the scheduled interview at AAA advertising.

The building which housed one of the leading advertising agencies of India had a few other offices in its compound, but the building in itself was a clear disappointment – cement patchworks, paint peeling off the fascia. It looked as if it had stood through many harsh seasons, though without much concern from the owner or maintenance team. Someone had rightly said that one shouldn't go by the looks and that someone was bang on!

Because once I was in through the glass door, the world turned around.

The air-conditioning was a welcome respite from the sticky heat of July. The reception was colourful and bright, with two-tone red and cream texture paint on the walls, a visitor section carved out of one end with brown sofas and a security desk on the opposite end.

The only element that mismatched this cheerful setting of the front office was the security guard. He would have been a hit hero in movies of the South. He had a big face with swollen red eyes, a thick moustache, a bulging belly, hairy hands and a rowdy look on his face.

It seemed that the agency has been feeding him well. A good sign for me... only if they employ me.

"*Kisko milna*, entry *karo*," he said as I approached him.

Now, I was sure that not only his looks but also his accent would get him some roles in the movies.

"I am here for the interview, guard saab," I stuttered lamely while taking the pen that he offered.

"*Kisse milna*?" He waived his thick, hairy hand at me, asking who I wanted to meet.

"I don't know?" I retorted as the guard was irritating me with his gestures.

Just as he was about to say something else in his incomprehensible language, the door adjoining to the guard counter opened and a beautiful lady came out and stopped just short of me.

The guard would have himself taken the first round of interview with me if there hadn't been this interruption.

I looked at her. She wore a black skirt with a blue and red top. The fit was snug on her chiselled body. I must admit

I had only seen such curves back home on a mannequin at Kailash readymade garments.

And here in front of me was a living, breathing mannequin with a perfect body and face.

I was stunned, spellbound with her beauty and sense of fashion that I had only seen in movies.

After all, how can Kallan darzi back home, who tailored my shirt and trousers, compete with this designer display.

I was feeling miserable in front of her, sinking deep into my small-town syndrome. She parted her perfectly pouted mouth and heaved a big sigh before saying, "Yeess! How can I help you?" Her voice was so sugary sweet!

"Umm, I am here for an interview. My name is Mohit... Mohit Chawla."

She raised one eyebrow, popped her eyes and said, "Oh yes, yes! But you are late. Where have you been?"

I made an effort to unlock my tongue, which was stuck in the jaw.

She checked me from top to toe, thinking of what to do with me.

"Ok, let me check," she said even before I could answer why I was late.

She dialled a number on the house phone, mumbled something in the speaker for a while, looked at me twice in the process, and then silently placed the handle bar back on the cradle.

She swirled around and signalled me to come with her.

I hopped behind her nervously, while she danced along in front of me, negotiating a long aisle which housed multitude of workstations and cubicles swarming with human heads and hums of voices.

She turned a corner, walked through a line of glass doors and opened the second last. "Just go and sit there."

It was a meeting room with a square table, a sofa and four chairs, the whole furniture tastefully done in teak red.

I occupied a chair in that square room and waited, strange thoughts popping into my head.

Where are all the candidates? I wondered.

I checked my watch on an impulse. I had been waiting for nearly an hour.

Why are they taking so long?

The sofa caught my eye, and I was tempted to lie down. *How about being more comfortable while I wait?*

After all, a little stretching on the sofa would relax my nerves. I looked around and yawned, and then looked at the door.

I would have continued the same and the sofa would have won eventually, so I stood up, denying sofa the opportunity.

Just when I decided to go and snoop around to where Miss Pout would be, the door opened and a sheep, an owl and a mouse came in.

Nope, the surrounding had not transformed into a jungle, nor had any animals rushed into the meeting room. They were gentlemen walking in, although with strange features and expressions.

Standing as I was, I greeted politely, "Good morning."

"Morning, Mr Mohit Chawla," the Sheep said while he and the Mouse adjusted themselves on to the sofa. Meanwhile, the Owl dragged a chair from the table and placed it on the side of the sofa, settling his thick fat bottom on it, leaving me to face all of them.

"Let's have introductions first," the Sheep said in a thick deep voice.

He was clean shaven with gold-rimmed spectacles, wheatish complexion and was very tall. So much so that when he walked in, he was bent forward owing to gravity, just as nature does to the tall slender coconut trees.

He wore grey trousers of god knows what make. I bet that for a man of his proportion, he must have gotten the trousers and white shirt tailored. Impressive, no doubt.

The Mouse had a thick moustache on a small face, black protruding dancing eyes. He was wire thin, average height, two or three inches shorter than me. By the way, my height is five feet ten inches, which is considered good by Indian standards.

He was drab in comparison to the Sheep, wearing a purple shirt which wasn't complementing his dark complexion, dark brown trousers which were half an inch shorter than the should-have-been ankle length, giving full view of the blue socks.

He must have kept the thick moustache to add some gravity to his persona, else had he not been here to interview me, I would have mistaken him to be a peon, moustache or no moustache.

"I am Ramakrishnan, Director Client Servicing," the Sheep said clasping his hands together and leaning forward on the sofa, depriving me the opportunity to gauge Mr Owl.

"The gentleman to my right is Mr Chinnan Ghosh, Head of Client Servicing in Delhi, and to my left is Mr Sanjay Kumar, AVP, HR."

The Owl's face broke into an affable grin when introduced and he leaned forward to offer a handshake.

I tentatively took his hand, but the Mouse remained seated, impassive throughout. He probed me with his eyes, although I made an attempt to acknowledge him with a nod. As we gazed at each other, his eyes said it all. He wasn't enjoying this a bit and had come to interview me unwillingly. There was something about his expression, hatred or suspicion or something else that I couldn't point my finger on.

Our eyes were still locked and just as I felt the Mouse was going to utter something, Miss Pout broke in and handed three copies of what looked like my resume to them.

Much to my relief, the Mouse diverted his attention to Miss Pout and thanked her nodding his head up and down, "Thank you Natasha."

So Miss Pout was called Natasha. Glad to know. *Thank you Mouse*, I thought.

I took the liberty to get an eyeful of Natasha again for a couple of seconds, I believe, when she turned around to leave, and then turned back to face the three gentlemen who were here to grill and fry me. Ramakrishnan's eyes were locked on me.

Gotcha! Mohit you had just been caught staring at the bottoms of a female by the company's Director. You fool!

"Tell us something about yourself Mohit, personal, not professional," he said, eyes still locked, crossing his legs, leaning back on the sofa rest.

Be confident Mohit! So what if you were caught watching a girl's behind by this fellow; it was hormonal not intentional, I thought.

"Aaah... I was born and brought up in Sirsaganj, a small town of Uttar Pradesh. My father works in a cooperative society, and my mother is a homemaker. We are two brothers, and I am the older one... Hmm, that's it."

"Okay, what does your brother do for a living?" It was Sanjay Kumar aka Owl's turn now.

"He is still studying."

And I am an insurance advisor who has nosed around for some business, happy?

"Hmm... here your resume states that you were in the life insurance business since the last two years. How well were you faring in this field? I mean, what are your accomplishments till now?" Mr Ramakrishnan picked up my resume from the table and it was now a couple of centimetres from his nose.

"Well, I have insured close to fifty people through my network in the last two years, and have been adjudged best advisor of the month thrice in this span."

"Then why do you wish to leave such a rewarding career?" Ramakrishnan raised his eyebrows.

"You are finding it tough now, selling insurance *winsurance*... aren't you?" The Mouse chipped in with a mimic tone to his voice, trying to perplex me, make me anxious.

The challenge got the better of me.

"Nothing comes on the platter in this world, as you know," I said holding the gaze of Chinnan, taking him full on, while Mr Ramakrishnan was still engrossed in my resume.

"I work to support my family and work hard for it. I don't worry about the results and outcomes."

I was not finished yet. The Mouse had angered me and I wanted to vomit out my feelings.

"Yes, I can continue with the insurance job forever and as a matter of fact any job forever as long as I have heart in it. And the reason why I am here is that advertising interests me and I would love to do this job."

My gaze wavered and I saw Mr Ramakrishnan looking at me with intent and interest.

"Mohit, as I see, you have passed Business Administration with Marketing as a major from ADBD Institute of Management Technology." The Mouse picked my resume with two fingers as if he had picked up some soiled diaper. Obviously he was far from impressed with my answer.

"Yes sir."

"What does ADBD stands for?"

When somebody asks me this question, it hits right below the belt. Why? Because it isn't a famous acronym like ISB or SPCJ, and moreover, if promoters of my college had been more sensible, they could have anointed a trendier name to the college.

"Aaah, sir it is Angoori Devi Bhagwan Das Institute of Management Technology."

Wow, wasn't it great! If the Mouse would have poked his nose further, I could have elaborated on who Angoori Devi and Bhagwan Das were.

They were the grandparents of Gyan Das and if he might have asked who the heck Gyan Das was, he is the crème de la crème of Sirsaganj. A businessman, who owned four cold storages and a cinema hall in the city. He had never been to school and that his chartered accountant advised him once that the best way to convert black money to white is to open an educational institute under a charitable trust.

That's how Sirsaganj got its first Technical Education College.

"At least they must have taught ABCD in ADBD," Chinnan said mockingly, and then he glanced sideways to the left, seeking approval on the sick joke he had just cracked.

No one gave him any footage.

"Okay, we have one more question for you Mohit, much to the satisfaction of my colleagues present over here, because for me, the interview is pretty much over," Mr Ramakrishnan had again placed his copy of resume on the table and was leaning back, hands on his head. Seemingly relaxed, he asked, "What is advertising?"

"Sir, it is a communication of a brand, product or service targeted to an audience with a promise to fulfil and satisfy desires, realize dreams, achieve realities, fulfil needs, to render joy and happiness." I took a breather trying to remember some jargons or describing words from the book on advertising and communication that I had read years ago while in college, with one eye on the Director's pensive face. "Via advertising, a brand communicates how it touches peoples' lives, simplifies, comforts, gives enjoyment and makes their life complete every single day."

It was quite a twist of tongue, but this was one question which had to be answered well to create an impression on the interviewers, and so I tried to implant as many words as possible. Although I must admit I wasn't able to recall many of the words from the book, so I didn't know how much I had succeeded.

I only hoped I had advertised myself well to these gentlemen.

"Well Mohit, it was nice talking to you," Mr Ramakrishnan was on his twos now, standing, giving nothing away from his expressions, towering, forcing all of us to stand. "We will let you know what we have decided in a day or two." He turned to his side and said, "Sanjay, I hope you have made some notes."

"Yes sir," the Owl aka Sanjay said flatteringly and they all went for the door. The Mouse cast a quick glance at me while going out.

It was useless to search for any clue from the Mouse aka Chinnan's expressions, so I didn't even bother to acknowledge him.

When I went out into the hullabaloo of the office, Miss Pout aka Natasha was nowhere to be seen, much as I would have liked to speak to her.

So I headed for a taxi with the Mouse troubling my thoughts and raising doubts in my mind, for the interview had lasted only fifteen minutes.

(III)

"I will not be able to make it buddy," I said.

Sameer and I were having dinner that very day in the evening at a dhaba near our house.

He didn't ask me even once on how my interview had gone.

I thought he had forgotten, so I decided to raise the issue.

"Don't worry, you will," Sameer said shoving a piece of paneer in his mouth.

Ha! Bloody I had faced the interview, totally fucked it up and my best friend... he was so sure of my success. Height of optimism!

"Basis what, they just interviewed me for ten or fifteen minutes, never discussed the salary, or even the job profile of this bloody marketing or client servicing role."

"Basis this that you were sending your resume to companies for the last three months for different positions, and you never got a call." Sameer rested his elbows on the table, hands up, fingers dribbling with paneer pasanda.

"Basis this that you had lost hope, ready to go back to Sirsaganj, and I... I insisted for you to apply to this position." With a sudden raising of the elbow and poking a finger at me, he continued, "When I saw this ad in the newspaper, I forced you to take a chance for the last time, and... you were called for the interview."

He was being way too dramatic. "It is my gut feeling," he retracted his elbow and jutted it again at me like a spring, "you will get this job, by the grace of god."

The net result of my friend's overdramatic and over-optimistic melodrama was that for the second time, I had to wipe the paneer pasanda curry from my specs.

Let's see buddy, gut feel v/s gut feel, I thought.

(IV)

"Sanjay, you remember, we both rejected the application of this... Mohit? How come his resume landed at the Director's desk?"

"I don't know Chinnan... I seriously don't," Sanjay shrugged and continued. "After all, you raised the manpower requisition and *you* have to decide whom to keep and whom to reject."

"Yeah, plus, we had already shortlisted the candidates the day before... you and me. What happened to that list? Has the Director given time for those candidates, Sanjay?"

"No, I went to the Director to seek time for that very purpose. His secretary is on leave, so I went directly into his chamber. But all he asked me was to call you to his chamber."

"Stop tapping your feet Chinnan," said the Director as he walked into the conference room where they were both waiting for him. Chinnan suddenly froze and paid full attention.

"My dear friends, what do you think about Mr Mohit Chawla?" The Director slumped into the chair at the head of the conference table.

"Boss, that's what Sanjay and I were discussing. We have a list of candidates that we had shortlisted and I was coming to you to seek your time for their interview," Chinnan said crackling his fingers.

"We will talk about that later. The list can wait... and will you stop tapping that foot of yours, Chinnan?"

The Director turned his head towards Sanjay, AVP HR. "What do you think Sanjay?"

"Sir, this guy doesn't even qualify as per the company policy."

"How come?" asked Ramakrishnan, raising his eyebrows.

"Sir, as per the policy, we only recruit candidates who have passed out of at least top twenty B schools," quipped Sanjay.

"And boss, this guy doesn't even have any prior experience in advertising," Chinnan was encouraged by the policy issue being raised by Sanjay.

The Director showed his palm to Chinnan while he leaned forward and locked his gaze at Sanjay.

"Who makes the policies?"

The Director stared into the eyes of Sanjay and Chinnan, and the room fell into a pregnant pause. Sanjay lowered his gaze to the table.

The Director was famous for his short fuse.

"Tell me," Ramakrishnan challenged.

"The company," Sanjay stuttered. "The Board of Directors....."

"Who am I?" Ramakrishnan was still staring at Sanjay.

Sanjay lowered his eyes, "The Director."

"One of the Directors, and if others too don't have an issue, do you have an issue?" Ramakrishnan showed the longest finger of his long hands to Sanjay.

He looked at them again. Nobody met his eyes this time. They had surrendered in front of the almighty.

That settled, the Director leaned back in the chair and slumped further into it, with both hands on his head.

"Well gentlemen, I have a good news, especially for you Chinnan." Both of them looked up at the Director, wondering what bomb was going to explode now.

"Ten days ago, I had a successful meeting with the chairman of the Terra group. As you are aware, the group is engaged in real estate, infrastructure and mining as well, both in India and abroad. Now this group is foraying into the telecom sector and will be launching the GSM and CDMA handsets in India." His words met with blank stares, so he continued.

"The good news is," the Director was now rocking his chair, "that I have already signed an agreement with the client. They have awarded us substantial business this year."

"Sir, what will the business total up to?" Chinnan interrupted, rubbing his hands together.

"We are not here to discuss the agreement, Chinnan. I will mark a copy to you as your team is going to handle this account."

Chinnan gargled with joy.

The Director continued, "The fact of the matter is, gentlemen, that the VP corporate communications of the client called me a week ago and requested whether we can accommodate a candidate for the job that we advertised."

Chinnan stopped making the gargling sound; the Director now had the rapt attention of his pupil.

"I didn't relent at that moment. In fact, I only said that he can send in the resume and I can arrange for an interview, nothing more than that." The Director had made his point very clear, Sanjay and Chinnan thought.

"Now tell me Sanjay, is it improper to oblige a client, when upon interview I find that the candidate can be given a chance to serve us?" Ramakrishnan asked, crossing his long fingers on the table.

Sanjay maintained his silence with the fear of another lightning to strike. It was Chinnan who spoke. "Boss, I am not saying that you aren't right, still don't you think employing this Mohit Chawla will bring dissonance amongst other employees? I mean, after all, all of us in the agency are from top institutions."

"Who said we would employ him in the capacity of Manager – Client Servicing, the post we advertised for? We can create a new designation, can't we Sanjay?"

Sanjay removed his glasses, thinking hard. Staring at them, he said, "Yes we can... whatever you say, Director."

"Good! Prepare his appointment letter, designate him Executive – Business Development."

The Corporate Vulture

(I)

I was bang on time, with the offer letter in my hand, facing the burly hairy security guard again. He looked at me as if he was examining a spec of dirt, then he raised his eyebrows enquiringly. I gave him the offer letter to read without uttering a word. Somehow, we both understood that sign language would be the best mode of communication between us as he raised a palm signalling me to wait and disappeared through the door.

I decided to rest my bottom on a sofa while I waited.

After about fifteen minutes, which seemed like eternity to me, the guard came back, waved at me and showed something scribbled at the bottom of the letter. It read: 'Meet me at the first floor – Chinnan.'

I went in and climbed the stairs to the first floor.

After enquiring the way around for his workstation, I stopped just short of the cubicle Chinnan was in.

He was bent on a newspaper which was spread on his table.

I peeped further. He was reading some article on how to prepare prawns in red wine and olive oil, of all the news that happened in the world.

Ha! In the middle of early morning, I had barely digested my breakfast.

I cleared my throat to gain his attention.

No response.

I followed his gaze to the newspaper. It seemed like that glass of wine in the picture in the newspaper had his full attention, not the article, and he was committed to do something about that in the near future.

"Boss," I said.

Those four alphabets broke his jinx. He turned and fixed his red eyes on me. "Nobody calls me boss here. It's either Sir or Chinnan, understood?"

I wondered why. Was that because, back in school we had a full acronym on that word. Hmm, what was that... 'brother of sexy sister' or something like that?

Was Chinnan really the brother of someone sexy? Might have been, that's why he felt offended.

"What are you staring at now?" he said in a sarcastic tone, fondling his tie.

That triggered me to examine his attire.

The only thing that was right in his whole attire was white socks on black shoes.

But then who wears a brown shirt on sky blue trousers and what's with the golden tie and brown belt!

"Is there anything wrong with you, Mr Mohit?"

No, it is with you, bugs bunny, I thought.

Apparently, I had no verbal answer to his question, so I kept mum. He gave me a disapproving look, tilted his head and shouted at someone behind me, "Yogesh, come here!"

A lanky man with shabby hair, a pointy nose and a bit better sense of attire approached from behind and occupied a lone chair opposite Chinnan.

"Yogesh, he is Mohit and he would be working with our team," Chinnan pointed a finger at me as if Yogesh would have missed a man standing at the door of the cubicle.

Yogesh squeezed his nose and looked at me as if I was a housefly perched on his pudding.

I tried to smile and offered my hand to him.

"Hi Yogesh."

He took my hand as if he was given a dead fish to hold, expressions unchanged.

"Come, I'll show you to your workstation."

So I followed him to where my workstation was to be, leaving Chinnan behind, who turned his head to that same page in the newspaper.

Yogesh took me to the ground floor and led me to a semi-circular area housing a bunch of workstations.

We steadily moved towards a woman seated with her face turned against us.

She wore a sleeveless kurta over rugged jeans, busy filing her nails on her beautiful, tapered fingers.

A strand of maggi hair, roving out of the bun, was exploring her right cheek, her succulent... Oh! Mind my language... juicy lips pursed in concentration.

Goodness me, she was a beautiful sight. So refreshing... Ah! Miss Pout.

"Arre Natasha, Chinnan has got a new man in the team," Yogesh said morbidly, as if Chinnan had caught syphilis.

Natasha turned, fixed her lovely eyes at me and said, "Hi!"

I smiled and started to utter 'hello' or something like that, but she went back to her 'all important work', without wasting time on pleasantries.

Yogesh pointed at a workstation right next to Natasha's and settled at the other end.

I took the seat. She was sandwiched between us now.

I looked at her from the corner of my eye; she was such a pleasant sight!

I could come even on Sundays just to be seated next to her.

She rolled her eyes and sighed.

Just a little sigh, out of the boredom I believe, then she murmured something to Yogesh; he nodded in agreement and they both left their seats in unison.

I was left stranded till the evening and killed time reading files on the computer.

After a few more hours, I felt bored of data and presentations, so I just happened to look around. I saw both Yogesh and Natasha standing at the stairs of the first floor; they climbed on and disappeared.

I waited for them to come back to their stations for over an hour, so that I could strike a conversation with them.

But they never turned up that day.

A day passed and then two... I was so desperate to get along, strike a conversation and get to know my colleagues.

But after a cursory 'hi' and 'hello', they tried their best to avoid me.

On day three, I decided to speak to Chinnan on the cold war treatment of my colleagues.

As I recalled, Chinnan had directed Yogesh to align me with work process and company systems on the first day, but Yogesh had studiously avoided me all along and Natasha was clearly under his influence.

They were behaving as if they were taking me to be a threat to their individuality and freedom, or as if I had come straight from the jungle into the bustling city.

I hopped on to the stairs and tried to get through to Chinnan.

I reached near his cubicle when I heard his high-pitched voice.

"*Kiiii... kiii..... eeeeehobenaaaaaa...*" He was trying to get through to someone over the phone.

He looked at me and waved as if he was shooing away a dog and continued bellowing into the phone.

That fuelled my curiosity to quite an extent. I thought I should see what the urgency of this man really was and peeped over.

His finger was on the computer's mouse... trying to click a link.

Net banking. He was trying to access the net banking window, but as the computer firewall had blocked the pop-up, he was not able to access the landing page. I am sure he had no clue on how to resolve it, and that's why he was going crazy.

Obviously, he was baffled and was asking someone for help, but wasn't able to explain the problem over the phone.

I knew how to resolve this problem. The yellow notification line on the top of the window was the solution. It was obvious that Chinnan was old school and was not completely at ease with this modern-age marvel, the computer.

"Excuse me, sir," I tried to intervene.

He again waved his hands in frustration.

Be with it then... Moron, I thought.

I spent two more days either stuck to the seat or loitering around the office. The behaviour of my teammates was very weird towards me.

Natasha was like a cool breeze, soothing on the eyes but a cursory 'hello' and 'bye' was all I got from her every day.

Yogesh didn't even bother to give any response to my greetings, so only a little was expected from him. He was very privy to his work, and treated me like someone who didn't even exist.

My conversation starters with them went in vain every single time. They posed to be busy, almost so burdened with work that there were times I felt guilty at disturbing them.

By the end of the fifth day, I had Stick Cricket, Solitaire and Farmville on my computer screen.

After all, I had nine hours of working, but nothing to work on. No one was guiding me, easing me into the new environment. It was all play time then.

As I was about to pack up after another useless day, I received a mail on my official mail id.

It was a mail from the Director for a review meeting to be held on coming Monday.

I noticed that the Director was fond of labelling work groups with quirky names. Like ours was the Star Wars group, and then there were Transformers, Avengers and many others.

Fancy that, Chinnan, the Mouse, headed the Star Wars and the Transformers group.

As I read the mail further, I came across an interesting aspect of Mr Director. He had called us for the review meeting over lunch.

It seemed he didn't believe in wasting a single unproductive second.

The mail concluded with '... champions of Star Wars and Transformers group, please ensure your presence on the given venue, expect no absences or delays from any of you addressed in the mail'.

So, it was the turn of the Star warriors and the Transformers for the review meeting on Monday.

My only concern, however, was of how I would sneak the tiny morsels of food into my mouth without catching the Director's eye. I let my imagination race. Was the Director a different person during meals or was he the grandma of the house, showering his affection and love to all of us? All of us, the Minions, chewing under his kind gaze. I tried to construct the scene. Well, it was a far cry. The Director was nothing like the kind granny; he was actually a tough nut.

(II)

I kept the whisky bottle on the table and noticed that Sameer was already home.

He saw me too, taking his eyes off his laptop screen. "Hey, what happened to the dear old friendly beer? And today is Monday baby, not Friday."

"I know, bring two glasses from the kitchen if you want to have some, and something to eat also," I said, collapsing on the cot.

"Hmm, you are adapting to the corporate culture well, haan," he said moving towards the kitchen.

Corporate culture, my ass. I was bitten by the corporate vulture today.

I followed Sameer to the kitchen; he fished out a packet of cashewnuts hidden somewhere in a jar.

Embarrassed on finding me in the kitchen peeping over him, he thought of giving me an explanation on the treasure trove he was hiding.

"Hehe, I kept it for the rainy days."

I made a face to that and we headed back to the living room.

We had the first three pegs in silence.

Sameer had judged my sombre mood and had kept his silence all the while, which was so unnatural, given his vocal and cheerful nature, especially during drinking sessions.

"I am taking another. You wanna have one more?" I asked, pouring liquor into my glass.

Finally irritated at the gloomy and sordid picture I was creating, he said, "Now would you tell me what happened. You look as if someone has fucked your happiness."

"Exactly, I have been verbally raped... no, gang raped to be precise, that too in front of the full forum."

I said and then unable to hold on my emotions further, I started narrating what had happened in the office that day over lunch.

The Director had taken us out for the luncheon meeting, all eleven of us, the Star Warriors and Transformers of his universe.

We sat in a private dining hall of a popular South Indian fine dining restaurant. The silverware in front of us was proof of how upmarket and expensive the restaurant was.

While we waited for the order to come, he asked to be updated on various projects and those that his colleagues were working on.

I was seated on the far left of the Director and was gaming on what would arrive early – the Director's attention on me or the servings.

My bet was on servings, as I would be spared the attention then.

Strangely, the Director skipped me even before the servings arrived. He simply skipped me as the lone soldier who survived his line of fire.

Maybe as I was barely days old in the company, and was not worthy for a feedback.

Then the food arrived, the full-blown cuisine – the dosas, uttapams, curd rice, rasam vada and kheer.

Sambhar was delicious and I helped myself to the dosa for the second time.

And why not! After all, the dosa was smaller than what I used to have in Sirsaganj.

And so what if the Director was paying 350 bucks for it! I have never paid more than fifty rupees for a dosa.

The chomping session went uneventful, for it would have been difficult for people to answer with mouthfuls of food.

It seemed that the Director was well brought-up and taught early in life that 'thou shall not speak while eating'.

The last spoon of kheer was halfway to my mouth when finally, the Director spotted me.

"So how was your first week in the company, Mohit? You are Mohit, right?"

I aborted my mission to guide the last spoon of kheer to my mouth and nodded in affirmation.

I looked at Chinnan impulsively, who was seated right beside the Director.

His face was impassive, but he looked at me with his flickering eyes.

I googled in his eyes, and the eyes said 'thou shall not trust me buddy'.

The Director's question had caught me in two minds – shall I tell him how these people are treating me?

I decided to sort it out with my not-so-dear colleagues gradually and not share it here, in front of everyone. More so, another team too. Discussing the behaviour of my colleagues in the open forum was not my piece of cake.

I was confident I would win over them eventually.

"It was fine, sir."

The Director wiped his fingers and mouth with utmost care, taking his time while I gorged on the last spoon of kheer hurriedly.

But then he was in no mood to leave the casual chit chat. It was evident that he was happy with the food and the feedback from the team.

"So, what have you been doing for the last five days?"

"Nothing sir."

I wanted to elaborate after a breather, but the answer wiped the smile off his face.

I quickly realized that my response had been point blank, the tone brazen, and perhaps too quick for his anticipation and taste.

That was a mistake; the Director had a very frail temperament, as I had heard.

Suddenly he looked at Chinnan with a pissed off look. "Why?"

Now when you have raised the question, screw his happiness, please, I thought.

The Mouse and his pet Yogesh had been treating me like an untouchable ever since I arrived in this company. So naturally, I secretly felt happy the way the Director reacted to my answer. He was not blaming me, but Chinnan, for making me do nothing since I joined.

"Boss I wanted to discuss this issue myself with you, one-on-one," Chinnan spoke.

Wipe the kheer off your moustache, bojo, I thought.

"What issue? Go on, tell me," the Director encouraged him, his expressions unchanged.

"I wanted to seek your advice, on his activities of the past week."

"Why? What activities?" The Director hadn't expected that the small pep talk would turn up like this and was visibly irritated.

"Sir, ask Yogesh." Chinnan was in eye contact with the Director. His voice had extreme honesty. I wondered what crap he had planned to unload in front of the Director.

"Yogesh tell him, what was Mohit busy doing all these days?"

"Sir, on Chinnan's advice, I had given him some case studies of our clients. We had asked him to analyse them and present them to Chinnan, but for the entire week, he was only busy on Facebook, Stick cricket, Solitaire and what not! I warned him many times," Yogesh said nervously, shrugging his shoulders.

I looked at Yogesh in surprise. It was a plain, goddamn lie. He never assigned me any work all this while. I could not understand what enmity they had with me since day one of my arrival. They were clearly victimizing me, and I didn't even know why.

The Director looked at me frowning.

"Is this true?" he asked in a strict tone.

I should have retorted immediately, but I went point blank, and my lips seemed glued.

"Do you understand the gravity of this Mohit? What you have done is a serious compliance issue."

He contracted his face in disgust and banged his fist on the dining table, "How dare you play games on the company's expense and time!" He then looked at every one continuing, "... and the brevity is that he is only days old in the system."

Blood rushed down to my legs. I was ashen. I had never faced such an insult in front of a crowd.

I gathered some courage to protest to the allegations.

"But sir," I said meekly and was surprised by the weakness in my own voice.

The Director pointed his finger at me, "No buts. I can easily take away the very job that you are taking so casually."

His engine was hot and I was certain that he would kick me out of the job if he continued like this. I needed a divine intervention.

It was not divine, but a swine that intervened.

Chinnan quickly picked a glass of water from the table and offered it to the Director.

That trick from Chinnan was to distract the Director. And he had been successful in his endeavour. The Director wanted to continue with his barrage of words, but as he looked at the glass full of water, he suddenly felt thirsty. He took the glass from Chinnan's hand and emptied it in two long gulps.

Chinnan re-introduced himself to the scene that very moment.

"See Mohit, there are no free lunches in this company. Nobody will spoon-feed you. You have to take the initiative yourself, else it would be very difficult." He addressed me in a reproving tone.

The water had soothed the frayed nerves of the Director and his tempo lost steam altogether.

Chinnan took this as another opportunity, "Boss, I wanted to discuss this alone. Sorry to have ruined your lunch."

The Director nodded in affirmation, as if he concurred with Chinnan and looked at me in disgust.

"Buddy, those scoundrels have all the tricks up their sleeve," I said with a slur after narrating the events to Sameer.

"Hmm... they certainly are pushing you off the edge," he said thoughtfully.

"Because it's no big deal. People are glued to Facebook and games on their mobiles all the time nowadays. What would the corporate do, kick all of them out?" Sameer reasoned.

I just shook my head in despair.

"Fight it out buddy, you will come across bullies everywhere in this city." Sameer sighed.

Third Grade Village Institute

(I)

I don't know what to call it—infatuation, physical attraction or love.

She was simply irresistible. I was drawn to her the very first day, dreamt of being with her, up close and personal, and here I was barely inches away from her in the Delhi Metro train. I couldn't avoid stealing quick glances at her. She wore a sleeveless red kurta over a pair of jeans and every now and then, her arm touched mine due to the movement of the Metro, sending shivers down my spine.

Her velvety razor-cut hair kissed her forehead.

She had those perfectly arched eyebrows, fluttering long eyelashes and a perfectly chiselled nose.

She was amused at something. Every now and then, there was a faint smile on her full lips while she texted away on her I-phone with her long slender fingers. Her act was a charisma in itself. I revelled in her beauty. She, on the other hand, was totally oblivious of me, and understandably so, because all the while she had paid more attention to the dustbin beneath her desk than to me in the office, although our desks were right besides each other.

"What are you smiling at? Is there some joke written on my face?" She suddenly asked, still fixated to the mobile.

"Err... no Natasha. I am just excited and looking forward to my first client call." I was slightly embarrassed having being caught in the peeping act.

She sighed, fluttered her lashes a bit more, arched her brows further and looked at me. "Look Mohit, I advise you not to utter a word in front of the client. Just listen and take notes for the minutes of the meeting, understood?"

I nodded my head in affirmative. After all, I didn't want to be on the wrong side of the fence with my colleagues after that episode with the Director. Nearly one month had passed since the famous bashing I had received from him. The grapevine of the agency ensured that within no time, everybody knew Mohit. So I got recognition overnight, but for all the wrong reasons. My dear colleagues started communicating with me via emails. Chinnan still remained inaccessible to me all through the month, so seeking guidance on how to or where do I fit in my role in the agency was out of question.

I was still an outcast by far, but then suddenly, later in the day, Chinnan called me on the desk phone and ordered me to accompany Natasha for a client call. Taking it as a platform to break the ice, I called Natasha for the client brief. After all, I needed the background and the story of the client, for which she reluctantly agreed, but also made it clear that I was getting this opportunity only because Yogesh was on leave for a few days.

It wasn't an international brand that we were going to for a business pitch; it was a local innerwear brand which Natasha was trying to win over from the rival agencies. Although our agency was truly an international one and big brands from across the world were in our kitty, but developing local businesses was also a requisite from branches in every city. Local brands helped in making the branches self-sustainable and also did some good to the bottom line of the balance sheets. Therefore, every group in the agency had a target for local business also.

We reached Jhandewalan, where the marketing office of NiNi undergarments was situated. The building was drabber than our own. We climbed a narrow staircase from the side of the building and that gave way to a slightly wider corridor. At the end of the corridor was an open door and there were hundreds of sacks piled over each other visible behind it. As we crossed the corridor towards it, I started having serious doubts on the sanity of Ms Natasha. The place wasn't meant for girls; it looked like a warehouse. With a quick-beating heart, we, I mean I, crossed the sacks and we landed in an open hall.

The hall was the hub of many activities; people were packing and sewing packaged material in sacks at one end, then there were chairs and tables sprawled over the rest of the hall. There were also people talking on the phone, taking orders and people on the computers making invoices. This really was the warehouse. Natasha crossed the mayhem without batting an eyelid as if she knew the place like the back of her hand. At the far end of the hall was a heavy wooden door. She knocked and pushed the door open, while I remained a step behind her.

"Hello Mr Gupta, how are you?" Natasha crooned in her special sugary voice reserved for clients. I wonder if he had diabetes, because if he did, the next half an hour would be lethal for him.

"Jai Shri Krishna, Natasha ji."

"Namaskar sir," I greeted him, as I stepped on the wooden flooring.

It was a large room with an all teak décor – teak walls, wooden flooring, and even the ceiling was wooden. Gupta must have spent a hell lot of money on this room. I am sure he was not left with anything for the makeover of the bigger hall we had just crossed, and that's why it was in such a state of chaos.

I understood which part of the world I was dealing with. He probably had piles of monies stacked in his treasury chest, but he belonged to the category of people who considered employee warfare better than employee welfare, given how sprawled and messy the rest of the office was.

Now, right in front of us behind an enormous desk was the giant Panda, I mean Mr Gupta. He sat on a high swivel chair which was a tad higher than the visitor chairs. There were two large wall hangings of Tirupati Balaji and Vaishno Devi behind him.

He gestured to us to have a seat, all the while maintaining a fake smile on his burly face.

"So how did you like the creative?" Natasha asked batting her eyelids.

"They are indeed good, Natasha ji but the celebrity is too flashy. You see, I am a small brand and I don't know whether this celebrity will gel with us," he answered.

"He would, certainly," Natasha assured in a sweet voice. "We at the agency have a view that this famous Bollywood celebrity would give your brand an instant recognition when backed with a strong media plan. Otherwise you are just another innerwear company offering the same products as others do. We can distinguish you through this celebrity only."

She stopped and searched for some cue or an impact of her statement on his impassive face. Finding none, she continued, "Don't worry Mr Gupta, you are dealing with a reputable agency, and we know our business well."

"Natasha ji... Natasha ji, I don't deny the reputation of your company. In fact, that is the only reason you are sitting here with me," Gupta leaned to his side, opened a drawer of his table and fished out a sachet of pan masala. Popping two spoonfuls into his mouth, he started again, "You see, my purpose is to increase profits, and given the turnover I have today, I can't spare a whopping three crore for this celebrity. Can't we work out on some alternative plan?"

"We have planned everything according to your advertising budget, Guptaji. It is the third time you are asking me for an alternative. This celebrity would take three crores for a three-year endorsement. I think you have missed that part in the presentation." Natasha reasoned again.

"But why would I be giving him three crores? Please renegotiate or find some other celebrity. Get me somebody who is effective and affordable so I can utilize the remaining amount in, maybe other media consumption or dealer incentives. It's my hard-earned money, after all."

"If you were uncomfortable with the celebrity, you should have clarified that when the deal was made," Natasha was visibly miffed with the sudden turn of conversation.

"All this while I was under the impression that you had a problem with the creative or the media plan, and you never ever mentioned the celebrity."

Gupta spat sideways, a mouth loaded of betel nut juice, somewhere under his table, wiped his mouth off a hand towel and said in a stern tone, perhaps having judged the edginess in Natasha's voice, "Natasha ji, can we have an alternative plan now, when it is clear to you?"

I thought I heard Natasha swearing under her breath, "Bloody fat asses with puny businesses."

When Natasha started to shake her head in a negative, I intervened or rather blurted out, fearing that my very first client call was going down in dumps.

"We certainly can come out with an alternative approach."

"And you are?"

I realized I had not introduced myself to the client, so I presented my visiting card to him humbly.

"Mohit, let us discuss what you have in mind amongst ourselves at the agency first," Natasha advised me authoritatively.

Gupta ignored her, now addressing me directly, "Go on Mohit. At least give me an outline of what you have in mind because you people would again take a month to prepare something for me and if I reject the idea, it would save you the trouble... the big agency guys as you are," he said smiling slyly.

I looked at Natasha, who gave me a warning stare.

"Oho, Natasha, let him speak. He looks quite talented to me," Gupta chided.

I don't know whether it was a compliment or he wanted to humour us; people like him sought pleasure in peeling sophistication off the corporate executives layer by layer, challenging their professional facade, their knowledge. I didn't want him to win in this.

I also knew that now we had a fairly slim chance that he would come to us. It was almost sure that he would go back to his old little agency, but I wanted to put some serious thoughts across to him.

Meanwhile he was taking pleasure suckling pieces of betel nut stuck somewhere in his teeth. His lips moved in a strange way, as if throwing small kisses to the air.

To hell with 'do not speak' policy.

"Sir, I completely understand your insecurities. It's not always easy to take a big step. It has happened in the past that these celebrities overshadow the brand itself, you know, or as in the case with this celebrity, they endorse four to five different products at the same time, so there is a high possibility that a small brand like yours would get lost in the crowd."

Gupta nodded his head in approval. He was a thorough businessman and knew well that he was a small brand.

I continued, "So how would you like to project your brand? The usual way like the other undergarment manufacturers do?"

Gupta raised his eyebrows above his puffed cookie eyes. Obviously, he was intrigued.

"A nearly naked masculine man, wearing your brand of underwear, saving a damsel in distress would do? Or an attractive sexy woman sparingly dressed, caressing a masculine dude suggestively would? Or something else?" I started tapping my lips with fingers and posed as if I was thinking hard. He stopped suckling and chewing on his masala and joined me in the concentration, Natasha gave a dramatic yawn, but I ignored that and continued, "Or rather what if I say that we project your brand as one of the honest brands which a common man likes to wear? What if people from different professions, like a doctor, an Army officer or an engineer endorses it, something like *'India pehenta hai'*... we surely can develop this idea."

Gupta grinned, showing his stained teeth, "Sounds good to me. I won't have to dole out a lot of money for endorsements, but from where would you find such people?"

"We certainly can work that out, can't we?" I looked at Natasha with expectations.

She gave me a hard, long stare and then turned towards Gupta. "Whatever my colleague suggested was purely his personal outlook. Please give us some more time so that we can redo the campaign for you."

Without waiting for a response from Mr Gupta, she rose from her chair, gave him a brief handshake, turned and walked away. I repeated the chore hurriedly and chased my beautiful, fiery and temperamental babe.

(II)

"Who do you think you are, the vice president of the company?" Chinnan asked.

"No Chin... Sir," I stood at the entrance of the conference room.

Chinnan had summoned me to his office. He was seated at the far end of the conference room, my beautiful, fiery and temperamental babe was to the left of his chair and Yogesh to the right.

Their eyes were set on me.

"Then who allowed you to open your crappy mouth in front of the client?" Chinnan blazed, pounding his fist on the table.

Ok, don't imitate the Director now, Mousey and at least trim the hairs jutting out of your nose when you come to the office next time, I thought.

"You haven't bloody even started to learn the nuances of the trade and you have the brevity to suggest your shit load to the client! You think we all sitting here are fools?" he shouted.

Chinnan had blasted at me the very moment I entered the conference room. The scene reminded me of the principal's room in school where he used to punish us at the far end.

"I thought we should give some engagement point to the client, so that we can buy some more time from him," I reasoned.

"Engagement point, huh!" Chinnan mimicked. "You bloody pass out from some third-grade village Institute."

I was taken aback by that particular comment on me. It was so humiliating. My eyes wandered off to all parts of the room, as I was not able to concentrate. I looked into the eyes of my nemesis who was staring at me. Our eyes met for a brief second and then she dropped her gaze.

I wondered what I was, the subject of scrutiny or the subject of amusement for these people? I had only tried to help her.

When I put forward the idea to Mr Gupta, it was not to insult Natasha. I didn't want to overrule her, she being senior to me. But honestly, things were getting out of her hands back there. After all, what did she expect from a small business owner. He wasn't like the marketing manager of a large corporation that she was used to dealing with. That client needed a middle path; he needed a big agency to boast of, but an affordable campaign.

What I deemed fit at that point of time, I did that, and also because my lovely lady was being cornered by the client. I was on her side all the time and if she felt that was me being rude, I was sorry.

I owed an explanation to Natasha, but not to Chinnan.

"See Natasha, I only intervened because I thought that we would lose the business. The way Gupta was behaving with you was not right. Still, if you think I have done anything wrong, then I am sorry," I said softly.

Although I saw her lips shudder, as if she wanted to speak, but it was Chinnan who realized that I had ignored him and had apologized directly to Natasha.

"Okayyy big guy, you think you are so good!"

I focused my attention to him; he looked at me with zooming eyes, nostrils swollen with anger.

I wondered why this fellow chewed on the issues, and never really swallowed.

I was sure he had serious anger management issues... maybe his wife ignored him all the while or his children didn't obey him. But whatever the case may be, I was his punching bag for now.

"If you think you have huge capabilities," he said sarcastically, "I give you a month's time to bring one client to the agency, on your own." Saying that, he smiled wickedly.

"Either bring a business on your own or put in your papers." He said the last words hastily, as if fearing retaliation.

None came. I was staring through him, incoherent, numb in the senses, he didn't matter to me, I would have resigned anyway if shit like this continued with me.

He poked a finger at me and spoke in the muffled hush voice, almost snake like, "You, my dear, have a month's time. Do you understand?"

"Yes sir." I turned and without looking back, walked out of the door.

(III)

It was getting dark outside. No, the day was not turning into night, instead it was still evening, still one hour to go before we called it a day and rushed home. Dark clouds settled in to cover the horizon, an apt reflection of my sombre and morbid mood. 1 licked my paws, literally, sitting on my workstation alone with the buzz of people around wrapping up their day's work. Natasha wasn't there, neither was Yogesh and I didn't want them to be on either side of me. At least not now, at least not today.

I perspired and felt hyperventilated, as if the air-conditioning of the office was of no use. I wanted to walk out of the office, to have a change of scene, wanted to come out of the depression settling deep into me, but then I didn't want to leave the building because clouds were threatening to rain any time and I had forgotten to bring my set of keys to the apartment.

On regular days, Sameer always reached home earlier than me, his office being closer to the place we lived. A cab dropped him usually by seven or, seven-thirty, while I always took the seven o' clock bus and reached by eight-thirty.

So I took to the terrace of the building instead. It had a small canteen which offered titbits like Maggi, samosas, patties, tea and other treats that one could enjoy. It was the favourite hotspot for executives craving for the so-called, intellectual talks over a cup of coffee and cigarettes. There were some who wanted to change the world, some who wanted to express their love for each other and others who were deeply involved in office gossip. They all thronged this place.

I had no desire to eat, so I walked over to the terrace railing, leaning over with my hands folded, taking in the warm misty air of the monsoon and looking at nothing in particular.

I thought I was alone on the terrace apart from the canteen wala, but then someone else caught my eye. I noticed a silhouette of a woman some distance away from me. With her back on the terrace railing, she also leaned over, facing the canteen.

She took to my fancy, as I watched her pretending as if I was still watching the horizon beyond.

A contrasting sight. She wore a beautiful sari on her lean figure, and had a lit cigarette in between the fingers of her right hand, a few inches away from her lips, left hand folded on her waist supporting the right hand in air, as if she was holding a gun the way James Bond did in the movies.

She brought the cigarette to her lips and took a long drag of it, then raised her head a little, curved her lips in an O and puffed away the smoke in perfect round circles. She was totally engrossed and enjoyed the moment, oblivious of her surroundings, it seemed.

After two more drags, inhaling the tobacco of the cigarette and then guided by the sixth sense that women possess of knowing they are being watched, even behind their backs, she turned her head to the side and looked at me.

I literally tore my eyes away, embarrassed.

The very next moment I was glued to her again, having taken a fascination for her.

She took a deep drag of the last puff, the golden puff, as my smoker friends say and blew out a thick smoket in the moist air, dropped the fag end in between her *chappals*, crushed the butt under her left heels and started walking... towards me.

"Hey Mister! What are you looking at haan? Haven't you seen a woman before?" she said in a husky voice.

No, you are a rare sight for me. I thought.

"No, I was just passing time," I blurted out the truth. She took it otherwise.

"So, am I your time pass?" She folded her hands, taking my statement as offensive.

She had a chocolaty caramel complexion, flawless skin, deep set pond-like black eyes with little hues of dark under, just close to perfect puffed nostrils and luscious lips. I wondered why she was spoiling those with tobacco smoke. She had some X factor in her appearance, which would make one look at her twice. She was a little agitated, somewhat angry, and looked at me with those puffed nostrils.

"I am sorry if I disturbed your privacy, but then there was just nobody else to watch here... and pass time," I said on a lighter note, and bared my teeth in a grin.

She eased her stance at that, and smiling faintly said, "So Mr time pass, are you a visitor or do you work here?"

"Oh, I am Mohit, Mohit Chawla. I work here in AAA Advertising."

"O ho... so *you* are Mohit Chawla," she said in a surprised tone.

"What... how... do you know me?" It was my turn to feel astonished.

"Don't take it otherwise but I had heard that some dumbo Mohit Chawla has joined the Star Wars group," she said quickly and then gave me a quick body scan, "but you look quite handsome for a dumbo."

"Thank you ji, this dumbo is flattered by your compliment," I said cynically but then regained my composure. "Are you also from AAA?"

"Yeah, you would come to me sooner or later with a client brief. I am Parvathi Thomas, the creative lead for your Star Wars group," she said and extended her hand for a shake. "Don't worry, I am not the person who perceives people on the basis of rumours."

She held my hand, a firm confident grasp, a warm comfy palm, and intriguing eyes. In front of me was an amazing woman, a woman who smokes, wears saris and calls herself Parvathi. I would have liked to see her some more. Indeed the agency had its sheer load of amazing women.

"Would you mind Mohit, if I take my hand back?"

"Oh! Sorry," I let her hand go, with a smile.

"Ok, see you around then." She gave me a nod and turned, walking confidently towards the stairs.

"Bye," I said as I stayed behind her and wrapped my hand on the railing again.

Then my thoughts came back to those few who didn't want to see me around.

Jugaad

(I)

"Will you drop me to the station on Monday?" I shouted, as I hung out wet clothes in the balcony that I had just washed.

"Do you have nice tee and jeans that you can wear?" He shouted back. I peeped inside. He stood in the middle of the living room, with only a towel draped around his waist.

I walked in holding a wet shirt, "By gosh, are you going for a bath?"

"Yes, so?" he asked with an amused look on his face.

I raised my hands in the air, to the heavens in amazement. Why? Because Sameer led a dog's life. No, life was not hard on him, but because you had to drag a dog for a bath. So, it was a very special occasion indeed if he was going for it in the middle of the evening.

"We are going for a party, and I want you to wear something nice and funky. It's the best party of the city buddy," he said while turning back to the bathroom.

"I hope I don't have to pay anything," I said while I walked back to the window, "and do you know buddy, somebody in our society has bought a brand new black Jaguar."

"Is the number plate 1001?" Sameer shouted from inside the bathroom.

"Yes."

"It has come to pick us up." He said that ever so casually.

"Don't tell me! Really?" I dropped the bucket on the floor, grabbed my towel and started undressing for a bath.

I settled most comfortably on the plush cosy leather seats of the Jaguar. "Wow! What does your friend do for a living?"

"Nothing, there are a few lucky ones who are born rich. He is one of them," Sameer said adjusting his aviators on the nose.

"It's already dark outside, why are you wearing those?"

"It's a style statement, you see. We are going to meet the high fliers of the society today."

"Hmm..."

"Don't hmm that. You need to learn this craft. Even if your undies are torn beneath, your suit should be impeccable in this city. You should have style... you have to fake it if you want to make it in this bad ass world."

I needed to change the topic fast before Sameer got into the top gear of his gyan session.

"Hmm, so what does your friend do anyway?" I was still curious about this wealthy man who was kind enough to send a car for us, so I changed the subject.

"Well, his father has business interests in mining, infrastructure, telecom, etc. His grandfather is actively involved in politics, and to top it all, my dear friend has a couple of IAS officers in the family."

"Hmm quite a power-packed family," I rubbed my nose and looked at Sameer. Only god knows and I know how nightmarish these past few weeks have been for me. I had run from pillar to post, huffed and puffed on every lead so I could get one client, just one client, however small, but winning over a client is a complex process and without help and guidance from my colleagues, all my efforts had gone down the drain.

This friend of Sameer looked influential, he could perhaps get me a job somewhere. Or else, I would request Sameer to talk to him regarding me. Maybe, just maybe, when I do resign on the coming Monday, I will not have to go back to Sirsaganj.

But first and foremost, I wanted to know what kind of friendship they shared. "Buddy, how the heck in earth's name did you meet this millionaire?"

"Yaar, this is the problem with you. You start counting trees rather than collecting the fruit. Just enjoy... why bother?" He looked out of the window.

I knew his tantrums well now. He had turned into a *pakka* Delhiite; he never gave full info in one go.

I kept staring at him for full five minutes and he gave up, "Ok, I met him in London, where I was for a project last year. We were staying in the same hotel, so we had that Indian meet Indian moment, we ate, and we boozed after that every day and finally closed the London chapter fucking a whore together."

"What? Are you insane? You fucked a whore, really?"

"Yes really, and I feel ashamed since then, you know. It was so hard for me to keep this sin within myself. It's so much better now when I have confessed to you," he said unemotionally.

No wonder that's what many of our Indian men do when left alone in the foreign fair-skinned countries, without the fear and stigma. What's social and cultural taboo in India is commodity shopping in foreign lands. I thought at least Sameer was a touché better if he felt guilty after returning, because most people don't.

"But don't get the wrong impression of my friend," Sameer tried to explain his friend's position. "He is a good human, although he is a bit of a loose nut."

Suddenly the car came to a halt, and in front of us was a large gate manned by a sentry. As I checked my watch, I realized that we had driven for close to two hours.

The sentry opened the gates and the car inched forward in slow motion on the gravel path. I rolled down the window on my side so I could soak up the surroundings.

On both sides of the gravel road was the large expanse of cultivated land and far off, almost a kilometre inside, was a building, a huge bungalow,

I had lived my childhood and teens off these farmhouses back in Sirsaganj. I had bathed, played with friends under the sun on these farms, but those were the farms of the poor, where farmers toiled for daily bread and butter. This was a rich man's farm, for leisure.

As we inched forward, a loud thud of rock music filled my ears.

In front of me was a huge white bungalow, decorated with lights. The driver turned left to the parking lot, we crossed the Audis, Range Rovers, Endeavours of the world, some even with blue and red beacons.

Where our driver parked the Jaguar, there was a truck with two massive generators humming silently, powering the loud music and the lights.

Sameer knew where to go. He crossed the front porch of the bungalow and walked through the side lane, which was filled with cacti and rose plants that led us to the back lawns.

Two women, dressed in floral robes, showered us with flower petals as we entered the gates of the back lawns.

We walked a small distance and then stopped. Sameer's eyes were trying to identify the host amongst some fully clad, some half-clothed guests.

I, for starters, tried to get an eyeful of the scene.

Sameer was right. It indeed was a high-profile party, and I was sure lucky to have landed up here.

Commoners like me have only seen the captures of the parties like these on Page 3 of English national dailies only.

A funky woman with orange hair operated the DJ console, right on top of the swimming pool, bang in between the large lawn.

The pool was shaped like a kidney. While some people gyrated to the music surrounding the pool, a few were in it; most of the women were in their bikinis, men were in shorts, some bare-chested, some with a tee.

To add to the skin show were hostesses serving liquor and food clad in bikini thongs and floral shorts.

Sameer nudged me. "Ever seen so many girls in bikinis. haan! Many of them are Russians," he said and winked.

"So?" I retorted, as I perspired due to nervousness, having arrived on the high-profile circuit for the first time in my life.

"Yaar, you get angry over small things. It is a beach-themed party and I have got shorts for us also."

Just as Sameer spoke to me, a bald and thin man with a long beak-like nose spotted us from amongst the crowd.

"Look! Sameer my friend is here." He shouted excitedly in a heavy-accented tone and ran towards us with wide open arms as if a train was chasing him.

He didn't hug Sameer though. He just locked hands with him, swinging them side to side, giving the whole welcome a gay overture.

"And you would be Mohit, right?" He hopped on his feet with hands wide open.

I clasped my hand behind in fear, "Hello sir."

"Mohit, meet my dear friend Satendra Bhadana." Sameer did a formal introduction sensing the awkwardness of the situation.

"Hi, you can call me Satty. You know, you don't get closeness in full names," he leaned over to me.

"Mmhmm," I said, as I stood straight, avoiding his breath reeking of whisky.

"Come, come, let's have some drinks, then we can talk," he ushered us inside.

"Hey beautiful!" Satty called out to the nearby hostess, who looked more like an Afro-American model to me, given her long legs and ebony skin.

"What would you like to have? Let's start with Margarita," he asked, suggested or implied, I don't know.

While he was busy placing the order to the hostess, I WhatsApped to Sameer:

who's Margarita?

Sameer: *Its a cocktail of taquila*

Me: *Nw wht is tquila?*
Sameer: *Daru Hai*

He texted and then looked at me with blaring eyes.

Satty took us to a quiet corner of the lawn, away from the hullabaloo of the party. The leggy lass along with another hostess, god knows from which country, tailed us with Margaritas and kebabs of the world in hand.

We settled on the chairs besides a fountain.

"So how's AAA treating you, Mohit?" Satty asked.

I cringed. The Margarita was sweet, but nothing beats the sour taste of good old whisky.

I looked surprisingly at Sameer. He ignored me and answered to Satty instead, "Bad, he is leaving for Sirsaganj on Monday. He thinks he will be better off there."

"Really... what happened?" Satty asked faking surprise.

"You know, usual stuff, bad boss, office politics, etc." Sameer said in a matter of fact tone, as if these were all petty issues.

"Hmm... shall I speak to Ramakrishnan again?"

I coughed in response. It was a shocker of information and I looked at Sameer with complaining eyes.

"What, why are you so naïve Mohit?" Sameer asked as he signalled the ebony female for another round.

"Whiskey for me, please," I said shaking my head in despair.

"What! Have I done anything wrong?" Sameer got furious at my reaction. "You think you are talented, and you got this job on merit?"

I looked at both of them and said, "Not done."

Satty looked at me and then signalled to Sameer, "Explain it to him."

"See Mohit, there are a lot of people here in Delhi, who roam around seeking a job with merit certificates in their hands. It doesn't work like that here. I had enough of your sulking around for the past three months for a job, so I spoke to Satty about you and he asked for a favour from Ramakrishnan regarding your job."

He took a sip from his refill and continued, "Satty, is the non-executive director of the Terra group, which has retained your agency recently. In fact, AAA advertising had obliged its client by keeping you on this job."

"*Jugaad ke bina yaha kuch nai chalta*, Mohit *Babu*," Satty said.

"Wow! I am the only one who doesn't know. My friend knows, and I am sure my colleagues know too, that I got the job on jugaad." I gulped my whisky in a single shot. "You know, now I understand why they treat me like a street dog."

"Offo, chuck it man! Now that you have got the job, you also show some attitude," Satty said, chewing chicken malai tikka.

"How?! I must get a client by Monday, otherwise I would face further humiliation, and I would have to resign."

"Ohoo, it's just a small issue! Why do I spend so much on networking parties? Come with me, I will give you the client," he shooed the hostesses away while he walked towards the pool.

We followed him to the poolside, where the party was getting hotter by the moment; couples were locked with each other, dancing in a trance, showing vertical expressions of horizontal desires.

Satty called a Russian girl, who was in the pool, "Sabina, come out!" He ordered me, "Mohit, give her a hand."

She came out holding my hand, wobbling, totally drunk. We took her to a corner.

"Where is Gaurav Thapar?" Satty enquired.

"Which 'hic' Gaurav Thapar?"

"Arrey, the one who was with you a few minutes ago."

"Oh, I 'hic' think he went to pee, 'hic' didn't want to spoil your pool, geee," she giggled, swaying back and forth.

"So kind of him isn't it," he scowled.

"What happened? Why are you all circling my girl?" A man with a heavy moustache came out of the bushes nearby.

"Tsk tsk Gaurav, there is a washroom inside, and you are peeing in the bushes of my lawn."

"Satty bete, the washroom should be here, right by the pool next time."

"Achha listen," Satty cut him short, "have you fixed an agency for your new township project?"

"No, why?"

"Ok, AAA is your new agency and this man here," Satty pointed at me, "would be servicing you."

"Na na! AAA is a big agency, I can't afford," Gaurav retaliated.

"Just where you have stashed the money, I know very well." Satty turned to me. "I will give you his contact number, talk to him when he is sober. Trust me, you will get his business."

Then he addressed Sameer, "Now you people enjoy. If you want to stay, rooms are open on the first floor for you."

"Gaurav," Satty said grasping Gaurav cheeks with his fingers.

"Yes."

"Take Sabina's hand."

"Hmm..."

"Take my hand," Satty said this time.

"Ok."

"Come let's go for a good time together."

With that, the three of them jumped into the pool and to my awe and amazement, all party girls and guests followed the host as the DJ struck a popular English song.

"Sameer!"

"Hmm ..."

"Where are my shorts?"

(II)

With a stride in my step, I entered the office with the contract and the creative brief of my very first client, courtesy Satendra Bhadana alias Satty.

Of course we stayed at the farmhouse that night after the party and thanks to my old middle-class virtues and upbringing, I nearly saved myself from losing my virginity to a beautiful female, who clung on to me for the rest of the night.

That night gave me some very important learning in life and the first learning was that the so-called pillars of the society weren't just boozing and it wasn't just some skin show. In fact, it was a great networking platform for them.

Gaurav Thapar needed some important contracts from the Government and Satendra could have helped him, so he was there. An old bureaucratic cow needed a departmental transfer, so he could mint money before he retired, and Gaurav Thapar could have done that.

So, somebody was there for somebody to scratch the back.

That day I realized the power of jugaad; it weighs more than qualification in the real world.

You must be in the right place to showcase your calibre, your talent and qualification. Somehow in India, if you don't have jugaad, your talent and qualification would go for a toss. Jugaad ultimately puts you in the place where you want to be.

Satendra was a good host; he made us leave only when we had had breakfast with him the next morning.

That morning gave me another insight of the rich and powerful. While I still felt awful at the fact that I got the job and the client owing to jugaad, Satendra told me how he had managed the Master's degree from a foreign university.

He was never the studious type, failed miserably twice in the board examination, so his father shipped him to England.

England offered him a lot more than studies – girls, night outs, booze, drugs... he did it all, saw it all. He was evicted from the college due to non-attendance and poor results, nonetheless he completed his four years making merry because money was no constraint, and he had a lot of it.

He was summoned back to India by his father, at last. Money came handy again when his father arranged a nice fake degree for him and announced that he had arrived with a professional qualification from the foreign lands.

"Who's going to check, when you are rich and powerful? After all, I am the one paying hefty salaries to the IIMs of the world," his father had said.

I went straight to Chinnan's cubicle, to announce that I have finally arrived on the corporate scene.

He was busy fingering his newly-acquired iPhone, eyes glued to the screen, tongue out.

"Chinnan," I called him, trying to grab his attention.

"Haan," he raised his eyes for a friction of a second, recognized that the call of his name came from a person who wasn't so important and could wait.

"Just a minute."

I obeyed his orders and waited for full two minutes while he managed to just stop himself from jumping on the screen of his iPhone. He gave varied expressions every second of the two minutes that I waited. Sometimes he would thumb the screen so hard, with his eyes jutting out, that I feared that they would pop out of the sockets. Then, the very next second, he would tilt the iPhone to one side and with that moved his mouth, tongue, and the buttocks to the same side too.

What was he trying to do? Damage the iPhone unsuccessfully? I could have helped him with pleasure.

"Oh shit shit shit," suddenly, he shouted in anger as if the liquid from his bladder was out in his pants.

"Bloody, I missed the high score again," he looked at me as if seeking consolation from me.

Then he realized that he was seeking consolation from a junior-most staff of the agency. I was only above peons and security staff in hierarchy for him.

"What are you doing here in the morning?" He kept the phone on the table, came back to his senses and enquired bossily.

"I just wanted to share that I won the challenge." My eyes wavered to the phone kept on the table. The subject of his excitement and agony a while ago was Bubble Safari, a game on his phone.

"What challenge?"

"That I have to bring a client to the agency, all by myself."

"So, what am I supposed to do? Dance?"

"No but err... you only said."

He raised his hand in the air to stop me from speaking further.

"I am highly obliged, Mr Mohit Chawla," he mocked, "but remember, you are paid for this job only."

He grabbed his iPhone from the table once more and said dismissively, "Now go and report to Yogesh. Don't waste my time."

(III)

I was not able to recognize her for a while. Her hair were tied up in a bun high on her head and she wore geeky glasses on her eyes, dressed in a simple salwar kameez. It was a very different appearance from when I had first seen her that evening.

"Hi Parvathi!"

She removed her glasses, looked at me and smiled. "Hello Mohit!"

At least somebody was there in the agency who smiled at me.

"So, you recognized me?" I said, just to start off the conversation.

"Ah, I never forget faces that ogle at me," she said smilingly.

"I am not like that and I wasn't ogling at you that evening."

"All men are like that and they never accept it."

"What can I say, then! I surrender," I said and laughed.

She laughed with me. "Its ok, we women are used to it. So, what brings you here?"

"The client. Yogesh sent me here to discuss the creative brief of the client."

"So, let's start then," she said getting serious.

I was about to take out the literature about the client from my bag when her desk phone rang.

She looked at the number flashing on its screen, made a face in disgust and picked it up.

"Yes, tell me."

Her dialogues were in monologues and I strained hard to decipher what was being said to her on the other hand.

"But you only told me ..."

"How many times ..."

"You have to explain ..."

"Let me have a meeting with ..."

"Ok... do as you wish."

She banged the receiver onto the cradle, visibly displeased.

She extracted the pin out of the bun and her thick beautiful hair flew down her nape and kissed her back.

A moment later, she cursed, and gathered her hair back again with her fingers. "Bloody chauvinistic pig!"

I wondered how many times in a day women do that with their hair. "Who are you talking about?"

"He always has his pants down in front of the client, no matter how much you support him," she said and tied her hair in a bun again.

"But who Parvathi?" I wanted to know who was the person behind her anger.

"Your friend Yogesh, who else."

"He is not my friend."

"Whatever," she shrugged and made a disgusted face. "The client says something, he understands something else, then he briefs something completely different and when the client scolds him, he blames me."

I was confused if this was the same Yogesh that Natasha and Chinnan were so gaga about. "I hope you are not the same," she looked at me and enquired with an innocent face.

"How can two people be the same, Parvathi?" I shrugged, "Test me!"

"Hmm ..." She reached for her hand bag and fished out a pack of cigarettes. "We will see. Would you mind if I go for five minutes?"

"No, I won't, as long as you come back," I said and picked up a magazine from the table.

We got down to business when she came back, back to normal. It took me an hour to explain what my client wanted, all the while taking in a whiff of tobacco and mint from her breath.

When we were finished with the job, she raised her hands high above her head and stretched on the chair, "So when do you want to show this to the client?"

"As soon as possible, maybe in a day or two." I looked away to avoid staring at her swollen chest and the struggle of the top button which tried hard to break away from the kameez.

She resumed her normal stance and reached for the cigarettes again. "Too short a time. What do you think, I have a magic wand here?"

"Hey, you just smoked barely an hour ago, it's very bad for your health," I said out of concern, and checked my watch.

"Who cares?" she said, making a face. "You guys think you can get away with anything, you show concern because I am a woman and you guys don't like the idea of woman smoking cigarettes. Isn't it?"

What could I have said, she was right in some way, although my concern would have been the same for a man. Speaking of men, it intrigued me of what were her thoughts about competition with the male fraternity, so I coaxed her. "So are you competing with us, the males of the world?"

She joined her hands in mocking apology, "No sir ji. I can't compete with the most shameless creature on the planet earth."

"Shameless?" I raised my brow.

"Yes, shameless, because we don't take out our instrument every time we see a wall, we don't go about urinating in public as you men do for public viewing pleasure and we don't roam the markets half-naked also," she said in a hurried outburst of words.

I looked at her face in amazement, "What happened, Parvathi?"

"None of your concern," she looked away. "I think we are finished with the meeting here."

With a heavy heart and soul, I walked back to my work desk, pondering over what she could have gone through in the past for having such strong views towards men.

Cloud 9

(I)

Sometimes life gives you nice surprises and one feels wonderful when these surprises come from people around you. It was one such surprise from Sameer one fine morning, which left me speechless and emotional. He handed me the keys of his black Yamaha RX 135, 5 speeds.

He knew that it was something I wished for since quite a while, owning this piece of machine.

What I couldn't afford ten years back, Sameer already had. His father had gifted him this bike on his fifteenth birthday.

And ironically now, when I could afford one, it was on its way out of production and was now dated.

I looked at the familiar superman insignia key chain. Both Sameer and I had very fond memories of the bike. He often used to take the bike to school, and I used to ride pillion. On our way back home, he used to take a u-turn to the famous girls college of our town.

He was always very bold, even back then, while I used to be shy. I always felt jittery and awkward when he spun around in circles on the road, targeting pretty girls. His first crush was Preeti from his colony and he would often try to impress her with his acrobatics on full throttle.

I feared she would complaint to our parents, but she never did.

I remember vividly even today how Sameer intercepted her one day while she was waiting for her auto to arrive. I rode behind Sameer as usual that day too. He asked me to step down, whispered something in Preeti's ears, to which she giggled. He winked at me and handed me two rupees as fare for the auto back home. In half-a-minute. I was in the auto and she was behind Sameer on the bike.

I hurriedly went down the stairs to look at the bike. Sameer followed me.

Although it had not been in use for long now, but was still in pristine condition. Sameer's father had taken pains to keep her like that.

I looked at Sameer with gratitude; he smiled at me and said, "She's all yours."

I hugged him emotionally, tears welling up in my eyes.

"But on one condition," I said. "Just as I share the house rent, I pay you for the bike also."

"Of course buddy, I am not giving her to you for free," he said mischievously.

I reached office on a high note. The world seemed different, and the roads seemed different because the view from the bike was different than the auto and the bus.

When I stopped the bike at the office parking, I realized that I had been singing a popular Bollywood number on top of my voice all the way.

I entered the office and beamed a smile at Hairy Sharan, I mean Hari Sharan, the guard at the reception, and he stood up and wished me good morning in return. Ram Bihari, the peon of our floor wished me, the sweeper wished me, Natasha smiled at me when she came, I greeted Yogesh and he gave me a cynical smile with an 'I know what you did last summer' expression on his face.

People in the agency had started acknowledging my existence and it had all happened because I had been working on my third client in a matter of two weeks. My first client was happy and he had recommended me to the second, and the third came after a hard-fought battle with the rival agencies.

I was in the game and roaring with confidence. That's what success does to you, and then that's how success changes people's behaviour around you.

Suddenly people become more welcoming, congenial. And that's what was happening with me; everybody changed their colours for good. From a useless nut, I became the important screw in the ship overnight.

I picked up the phone to say 'Hi!' to the only colleague with whom I had developed a rapport over the past few weeks.

"Hi!"

"Hello! Wow, on time today," she said

"Yes, what's your plan? Let's meet in the canteen after thirty min."

"Ok, Chow chow," she said with excitement in her voice.

I smiled as I kept the phone on the cradle.

Parvathi looked like a tough nut on the outside, but she was a child within. Our friendship developed over countless formal sessions of client briefings. I discovered that she was easy to talk to and had no hang-ups, barring one touchy issue of male predominance. She also seemed to enjoy my company, so the formal sessions converted to informal tea breaks where we discussed a plethora of subjects, shared our views about new campaigns, clients, colleagues and the company and it was the unsaid rule to not touch the personal aspects.

I felt we both were lonely, with no friends in the office, so we struck a chord.

Time flew by like a breeze at the office and I stuck to my routine over the past few weeks, which involved stealing quick glances at Natasha time to time. I couldn't resist that leisure even if I tried hard not to. I was spellbound with her charisma. She was always impeccably dressed, ravishing and beautiful. I never found her with an iota of tardiness, no matter what day it was and what time. She always looked fresh like a rose, as if she had just come out of the shower.

She was at the back of my mind, playing with my mind all the time. Honestly, it was hard for me to sit tight when she wasn't around. I felt restless. I felt chaotic without her presence around me. Weekends became boring and I longed for them to get over so that I could be in office. She was the reason why I wanted office timings to stretch from nine hours to twenty hours. I wanted to be around her twenty-four hours, to bask in her glory.

There was one day in the past week when she was on leave and it was so hard to be in the office without her in the seat next to hers. That day it felt like somebody had taken the juice out of me; nothing felt well, not even the joke cracked by Parvathi during the tea break. That day I felt bored, irritated and broke as if I had no ambition in life and that day I realized that I felt excited to come to office just because Natasha would be around. I was totally fixated on her and was totally smitten with her.

But alas, she was totally oblivious of my condition.

Old and vintage machines have a mood of their own and I got a taste of it in the evening. Her engine had greeted me with a resounding purr in a half kick in the morning, but then in the evening, she was as dead as a stone even after trillions of kicks, a sore foot, perspiration-filled face and soaked undergarments.

I wiped my face with the handkerchief, mentally calculating the distance to the nearest mechanic when the next surprise came.

A Skoda Rapid came to a stop near me, I gave an exhausted look at the car and saw Natasha behind the wheel.

She rolled down the windows, "Nice bike man! Does it work or is it just a piece of junk?"

I gave my bike another try in response, and surprisingly, she purred to life.

"She is fine, but this baby has a lot of attitude," I said out loud over the thud-thud of the engine.

Natasha signaled me to turn the keys off and I killed the engine, hoping she would not trouble me again.

"I hope she would be in a better mood tomorrow," Natasha said with a charming smile.

"Sure she would be, but why are you asking?"

"Because you have to pick me up tomorrow morning from my house. We have to meet Gupta of Nini Undergarments again and he insists that I bring you along."

I was dumbfounded for a moment because of this sudden twist of fate this evening. I quickly found my tongue, "Are you sure you want to go on a bike?"

"Why? Will she mind sharing you with me?"

"Not at all, she would be delighted rather."

"Then 8 o'clock it is. Have your breakfast at my place tomorrow," she waived her hand and moved ahead.

I pinched myself to believe that it wasn't a dream. No, it wasn't, and then I kissed the tank of my bike in exhilaration. She sure was a lucky babe, after all.

Sleep eluded me that night, I twisted and turned on the bed and tried hard to shut off my mind and body so that I could get a good night's sleep and wake up fresh tomorrow. But the excitement building within me was overriding my sleep, my mind was conjuring scenarios, the visit to her house tomorrow, how would that be? What would she be wearing tomorrow? What would it be like riding with her on the bike? I had always dreamt of the day when I would be riding my bike with a girlfriend behind me. Natasha surely wasn't my girlfriend, yet, but it would be my first ever experience when a lovely lady whom I admire would be sitting behind me on a bike.

A ping-ping of message tone on my mobile interrupted my chain of thoughts. Natasha had sent me her address with *'see you tomm. Good night, sleep tight'* and a smiley.

I reached Vasant Vihar, one of the posh localities of Delhi, on time the next morning. It wasn't hard to find her brick red bungalow, but it was way more difficult to find the call bell on the huge front gate. It took me a few seconds to locate that. I pressed the button and instead of a usual ting tong of a bell, I heard a deep thick bark of a dog from somewhere inside the bungalow. I was amused and had a small mental laugh thinking that they have a dog's bark as a call bell. How unusual! That's when I heard the bark again, now loud and clear, closer to the gate. A middle-aged man opened the side gate and looked at me questioningly; a Doberman lurked behind him, barking relentlessly.

"I am here to see Natasha," I addressed to the salt and pepper haired man but looked at the dog whose barking had turned into a growl with full display of canine fangs.

"Ok, wait! Natasha baby has told me about you, but let me chain Coco first. She is in a bad mood today," the salt and pepper man said motioning at the dog, who was trying to leap on me from behind the man.

He escorted me to the drawing room after getting rid of the dog; the drawing room in fact was part art gallery, part museum to me.

I looked around with awe, soaking in the paintings, murals and artefacts as decorations in the huge room. My head started to spin, so I looked down at my soiled shoes on the white kota stone floor, just to get the semblance of the situation. I had been to the rich man's house of the rural and now I stood in the rich man's house of the urban. I bet the rural cousins can never match up to the class and show of the urban ones, no matter how much monies they had stashed in their pillows.

The salt and pepper-haired man ushered me to the semi-circular sofa set which was three steps down in the middle of the room.

The sofa sucked me in, the salt and pepper-haired man disappeared and a maid brought me a concoction of juice and then another brought a full volley of cutlery, full plate, quarter plate, bowls, fork, spoons, etc.

The maid placed the cutlery in front of me on the carved wooden table, eyes down, working deftly. Another one came, the original one who had given me the juice, holding a huge tray full of edibles. She placed the edibles in front of me quickly and she too disappeared.

I was alone in the huge drawing room now and in front of me was a pompous display of assortments as breakfast – fruits, sandwiches, pasta, paranthas... sumptuous.

Frankly, I was hungry, very hungry when I reached her place, but I lost my appetite soon after. Everything was so quick and mechanical as if the staff had been instructed to treat me exactly like an odd carpenter or a painter who had been offered tea in the house.

I grumbled. I shouldn't have come here... she was rich, filthy rich, but then this was sheer arrogance. Is it a way to treat a fellow colleague? She could have come to greet me at least.

I would not be eating all this. I could have had horseshit if she could have comforted me in her house. I am not a beggar seeking alms, and it is no way to treat a guest. Thoughts came up in my head randomly.

"Hi, what happened, you aren't taking anything?" A sweet chiming voice, which I recognized all too well, startled me.

She stood at the edge of the sofa. Somehow, she had tiptoed besides me when I was sulking.

I looked in her eyes full of kohl and forgot everything because she as usual stunned me with her appearance. A blue denim pee cap on her head and a blue jumper over a sleeveless orange tee, she was all decked to go for a bike ride.

She looked at me quizzically. "Is everything alright? You look constipated to me," she said patting her tummy.

I realized that the sulk in my mind was still pasted on my face.

"Come on yaar, this is just too much for me," I said casually, indicating at the lavish spread on the table.

"But I thought you would be hungry," she said faking a surprise.

"What do you think I am?" I raised my eyebrows managing a small smile. "Tarzan or Mowgli?"

With one hand on her small waist and a slim finger of the other on her lips, she pretended that she was thinking hard on the choices that I had given.

"I don't like any of them. I like 'Phantom', you know, the ghost who walks." She said smiling and mischievously looked at me.

"Are you kidding me, he was one of my favourite super heroes," I said in excitement as she came and sat beside me on the sofa.

"He is my favourite character too," she said picking some fruits off the table. "I like the mystery around him."

"Yeah, unlike any other super hero; he does not have any super power, but he is fearless and intelligent," I said attacking the parathas.

"And what about her wife Diana, she is so beautiful," she said laying more emphasis on the word beautiful, so it actually came out from her mouth like 'beeeaaauuuutiiifuuuullll'.

I looked her in the eyes, "Yeah, just like you."

Her face turned to crimson, she fluttered her eyes and dropped her gaze to the lone grape in her fingers. "I didn't know you were a great fan of comic books."

"I love reading them even today," I said trying to figure out which item on the breakfast menu was more delicious than the other.

We continued our talks on various characters of the comic world, while she pecked on the fruits. I, on the other hand, attacked everything on the plate.

By the time we were over with our discussion on our mutual passion, nothing was left on the table.

Finally, the moment arrived when she placed her hand on my shoulder to adjust herself on the back seat of the bike. In a matter of seconds, we were cruising on the road. I was cautious of her presence on the pillion seat and drove at a moderate speed of 40 kilometres per hour, negotiating the potholes and breakers on the road, an effort to avoid using the brakes suddenly.

I didn't want to put her in an awkward moment when one applies the brake hard on the bike and the pillion comes skidding forward, pasting herself to the back of the rider. It was an age-old trick boys used when they would ride their bikes with their girlfriends sitting behind them. There is a certain thrill in that, but she was not my girlfriend. She was a female colleague and I was trying to maintain her courtliness, least she gets offended.

She tapped my shoulder after a while, "Is this the max speed of the bike?"

"No."

"Then give her some respect. You are riding it like a bullock cart and I am really bored. Come on, give me some adrenalin rush," she said out aloud.

So my idea of maintaining her courtliness was wrong after all. I shifted into a lower gear and gave the accelerator knob a twist. The two-stroke engine of the bike responded with ease and in no time, I zipped ahead at 80 kilometres per hour.

"Yeeeehoooo!" She cried out in excitement from behind me. I checked in the rear-view mirror, her hands were in the air and she was super excited like a kid.

I saw a red light ahead and braked hard. She wrapped her hands on my shoulders to negotiate the forward thrust and I felt her full weight on me. Her body was pressed on mine leaving no space for even air to pass through. I smelled her fragrance, so near to me, leaving a tingling feeling down my spine and butterflies in my stomach.

The bike came to a halt, she adjusted herself quickly, then leaned forward and said in my ear, "Wow, you know Mohit, this is my first ride on a bike."

"Really, you have never been on a two-wheeler?"

"Nope," she said, "haven't even ridden a cycle ever."

"Why? You couldn't afford one?" I joked putting the bike in the gear again as the light turned to green.

She laughed throwing her head back, "Always been in the car. In fact, I got a car of my own when I was fourteen."

We covered some distance in silence, I checked in the rear-view mirror to know what she was doing in silence.

She looked around side to side with interest, and then our eyes met.

"Wow Mohit, Delhi is so green and the morning air is so fresh. I never noticed that in the car."

"Mhmm, that happens. I also found that out now, riding on the bike in Delhi. Till now, I also had only the restrictive view from the bus."

"How is it, riding in the bus?"

"Well, I can differentiate between thirty types of armpit smells now," I said as I looked at her.

She squeezed her nose in disgust. I laughed and focused my eyes on the road ahead.

Then on a hunch, I looked in the rear-view mirror again. There was something fishy in the traffic behind us. A particular car, an SUV behind us, had been following us ever since the last red light.

In order to clear my doubt, I took a sharp turn ahead and saw that the car continued to tail us. Now I was sure that need for speed of my beautiful female company had attracted three rowdy looking youngsters from the last red light.

I slowed down so that they may pass, but they also slowed in tandem and confirmed my suspicions.

"Why have you slowed down? It was fun." Natasha asked.

"Some men in an SUV are following us, and I don't find it right. They look like hooligans."

"Huh, tell me something new. I face it every day. When I am in the car, men follow me on the bike," she said unconcerned. "Now when I am on the bike, they are following me in the car."

"Yeah, I know it's so risky living in Delhi, when you are a woman and that too a beautiful one," I said in a matter-of-fact tone, "but don't worry. I know what to do."

I increased the speed of the bike and then asked her suddenly, "You know any coffee house nearby?"

"Why? I think there is one half a kilometre ahead."

I increased the speed further; the SUV followed suit honking continually, and tried to keep pace with us. I spotted the coffee house some fifty metres ahead and applied brakes with my entire might, turning left on the road. The bike screeched to a halt right at the door of the café. The SUV was still speeding and it cruised past us. Natasha and I stood beside the bike when they crossed sneering at us. My eyes followed the car to see if they still wanted to pursue us. They didn't as the traffic moved fast and they didn't have the opportunity to corner the car.

On the rear glass of the car was a vinyl sticker 'G****R BOY', as if they were the endangered species and needed to be labelled.

So far so good, I had foxed them and I didn't want them to be waiting for us ahead, so I grabbed Natasha by her arm and said, "Let's get inside. We will have some coffee and then we will move."

I chose a table by the glass wall, facing the road, and ordered café latte for both of us.

By the time our order arrived, it had started to rain outside.

We sipped our coffee in silence, and looked outside through the glass wall at the hustling and bustling of people trying to evade the heavy showers.

Then I remembered, "I think you should call and inform Gupta that we would be reaching late for the meeting."

"Naah," she waved her hand in the air, "not required, there wasn't any meeting in the first place."

I dilated my eyes in wonder, "So you literally were taking me for a ride, girl." Then I raised my hands in the air amazed, "I mean, pun intended."

She fluttered her eyes and looked at her perfectly filed nails, looking absolutely adorable.

"Why? You don't like taking a girl on a date."

My heart jumped when I heard that. So she really wanted to date me after all, the girl of my dreams.

"Why wouldn't I?" I said and tried hard to control the excitement in my voice, "Who would not like to date a girl like you Natasha, but then it was so unexpected. I didn't know you had a liking for me."

She leaned over to me from across the table, closing the distance between us, "That's what I like about you Mohit, the old-world innocence. You are different from the others. Guys make a pass at me all the time, trying to impress me and it's so irritating."

She relaxed and took a swig at the coffee, licked her upper lips to gather the froth and continued to speak her mind, "You are different because I know you have had a feeling for me but you never approached me, never made a pass at me."

"Because most of the time I was so stunned in your presence," I said motioning the waiter for the pay cheque with my hand. "You are a diva to me, Natasha, and I realized that I am no match for you. It's not always that you get what you like."

"And that's what makes you a sweetie pie," she said and grabbed my cheeks with her fingers, like a teacher would do to a toddler.

My heat skipped a beat on her sudden move, and my face turned crimson. She looked at my face and had a good laugh, then I joined her in the laugh.

We both felt that we had unburdened ourselves laughing at each other. I felt so light, so purposeful, as if I had a new meaning to life and a new purpose to live in Delhi.

"So where to madam, we have a full day left and the rain has stopped," I said bowing my head to her theatrically once we were out of the café.

"Let's go to Old Delhi, Delhi Fort," she said excitedly.

"You really want to go there? It would be so muggy on those narrow streets."

"Oh, come on! I have heard food is just awesome there. Besides, I have never been to that part of the city."

"Why, you were born in Delhi, no?"

"Yeah, born with a silver spoon," she said smirking, "which means I always got everything, even if I didn't ask for it, from the best places around the world."

"Which is good, perfect life for a beautiful girl like you, no?" I said flatteringly, adjusting on the seat of the motorcycle.

"Only if my parents had more time, for the little adventures with me. Most of the time my father is out on business trips, mom is a socioholic, and brother studies in the US."

We reached Nai Sadak while she continued with her raving, feeling more comfortable as she sat just a hair-breadth away from me, her face close to my ears.

"Which means that most of the time I have my dinner and breakfast alone, otherwise I can have anything which money can buy."

"Hmm," I uttered, genuinely feeing her loneliness. I tried to understand the perspective of my little lonely diva.

I stopped in front of a famous aaloo tikki stall. There was a lot to explore and a lot to eat from this part of the city. We had a lot of time with us, but then time slipped quickly, like sand slipping through our hands, as we explored the lanes of the walled city, the first for both of us. Natasha was amazed by the variety of things on offer by the shopkeepers in small cramped spaces, and more amazed by the tranquil, happy faces of shopkeepers operating out of small corners. I felt more like at home in this part of the city. I saw people with less ambition and more satisfaction on their faces.

Finally, we reached her home in the evening, exhausted from our little escapade.

I undid my helmet as she stepped down from the motorcycle.

"What about the office, shouldn't we inform?" I asked her.

"Don't worry, I will handle that. Nobody questions me." she said and looked in my eyes purposefully and suddenly planted a kiss on my cheek. "Thank you Mohit, for a wonderful thrilling day."

Then she ran away to the gate even before I could respond.

I started my bike in exhilaration. The sweet sensation of her kiss tingled on my cheek.

Finally, I had arrived on the love circuit, boarded the love train with a woman of my dreams and was heading towards cloud no 9, I thought.

That was my state of mind; I was on cloud 9.

Bullshit Ideas

(I)

It was a beautiful evening. A gentle breeze caressed my face, just a nip of cold in the air indicated that Delhi had left the sweltering heat and humidity behind and was about to enter the season of festivities.

Sun receded behind the horizon and looked like an orange candy, bidding adieu till dawn tomorrow. It indeed was a breathtaking view from the terrace canteen of our office building.

I felt tranquil and calm. After all, life had been treating me well and luck was on my side. I never had a bad field day since last few weeks. So much so that everything I touched turned to gold. It was that phase in my life when days turned into nights and nights gave way to the day quickly.

Days were meant for work, mornings and nights were dedicated to Natasha. We would talk at ends till wee hours of the morning, on issues as important as work to as trivial as to what she wanted to wear tomorrow, to what I had eaten for dinner. I was so engrossed in her that everything else looked secondary to me. Mom started complaining that I wasn't calling her as often. Sameer went away for a long-term project to London, and with him not lurking around at home, I got more obsessive and compulsive towards Natasha. I laughed when she laughed, I sang when she sang and when she wasn't around, I thought what she was doing, so I picked up my phone more-often-than-not and called her.

There were times she didn't respond or her phone was busy and I felt that anxious pang in my heart – why isn't she taking my calls? Whom is she talking to? Is there someone else in her life? But then, all those questions were washed away as soon as I heard her voice. I was so addicted to my phone that the mobile company that I subscribed to upgraded me from being the regular customer to a premium one and why wouldn't they? They were the net gainers with half of my salary going down the earpiece.

All that said and done, I still couldn't judge how Natasha felt about me.

Where was I in her frame of things? Because I was still hovering on the border line of being just a colleague to her boyfriend, and sometimes of being her lover.

She was temperamental and everything depended on her mood and the environment. So when we were at office, I was always just a colleague.

When we went out shopping or just on a leisure walk in Connaught Place, she would hold my hand as girlfriends do.

When once we went to a disco, no holds barred, we danced to the tune of music, just as lovers do.

Though I wanted to take our relationship further, I was in no particular hurry. I wanted to give her enough space and time.

Too early into the confession spree could ruin our nice companionship and while the agency paid me the salary to work, she was my fringe benefit to continue to work there.

Fringe benefits count more than the salary to keep your motivation up, especially when you are a punching bag for your boss.

I ordered for a coffee.

"Make it two," a husky voice called from behind me.

I turned around and saw Parvathi smiling at me from a distance.

"Hi!" I greeted her with a small smile.

She made a stance like a dancer poking fingers at the audience after the act, "Caught you today."

Then she came around and dragged a chair opposite me, "Keeping busy haan?"

"Yeah I was," I lied looking away from her. I had not met her in weeks. Earlier I used to run up to her, to discuss every little detail, then we used to meet in between for coffee breaks, but now I emailed her the work and she got that done. Technology is a great facilitator, whether you know somebody or you don't, you have met somebody or not. It doesn't matter if that somebody is in the same office or five continents apart, you can still get your work done via email. I wasn't avoiding her intentionally though; it was more to do with my state of mind, and its dreamy thoughts.

Our coffee arrived and we sipped in silence for a while. I still hadn't looked at Parvathi straight in the face and tried to avoid her constant stare, for my mind was point blank, and I searched for something as a conversation starter but couldn't think of anything to speak to her about.

I was getting reclusive and withdrawn day by day ever since the love flu had caught me.

Earlier I used to be so bubbly and chatty with everyone, but now I was always in a dreamy haze.

I cursed my uni-directional mind, which could only think of Natasha, the feeling which I could neither confess nor advertise in front of Parvathi.

Just when I was about to start the conversation on weather, like strangers do when they meet each other, Parvathi dropped a bomb.

"Are you married, Mohit?"

"No, why?" The question jostled me out of my stupor.

"So, do you have any relatives here?"

"No, you know I have only Sameer, my friend, and he too is in London now. But why are you asking this all of a sudden?" I was quite surprised.

"Nothing, it's just that I saw you in a mall with a woman and kids this weekend."

I nearly spilled the coffee on my shirt when she said that and looked at her in shock.

She raised her eyebrows and twisted her lips to one side, as if she had found amusement in my shock. "So who were they?"

I spooned my already cold coffee for a while just to buy time to decide whether I should tell her or not. It wasn't hard to remember where I was this weekend, but the question was how well she would digest the truth, because if she would not, I would be in big trouble.

I decided to tell her anyway. I was confident that she would not gossip around in the office.

I raised my eyes from the coffee and looked at Parvathi. "The woman was Chinnan's wife and those two little brats were, of course, his sons."

"Oh my god!" She said out loud and raised her hands to her mouth and then looked at me with round fearful eyes, "Are you?"

I knew what she was trying to say even before she completed.

"No no, I am not having an affair with her, for god's sake," I said laughing while she still held on to her expression of shock.

"Chinnan asked me to accompany her for shopping as he was busy in some meeting," I explained.

"So, you were playing porter for them with all those shopping bags in your hand!" she sighed and rolled her eyes. "Don't you see he was using you for his personal work?"

She sipped her coffee thoughtfully and continued, "What kind of meeting would be there on a weekend except he went somewhere boozing around with his friends."

"Oh come on, he asked me for a favour for once," I lied because he was using me for his household work almost every weekend on some pretext or another. I wasn't going to tell her that I delivered mutton and vegetables to his house last weekend while he was out.

"But you should have said no. After all, you are not his personal servant; the company is not paying you for all that. He is just your boss." She reasoned raising her voice a notch higher, visibly irritated.

"Come on Parvathi, leave it na. I don't have any issues with all that. I just want to be on his right side."

She looked at me as if she had not understood what I was trying to say.

"See, he still doesn't treat me as a part of the team, even though I am doing well with business. He creates some nuisance or another to drag me into it, so I want to keep him happy. It's just that I don't want to lose my sleep over what nuisance he would create for me tomorrow. So that's why I said I don't want to be on his wrong side."

"In that way, you will never be his favourite as long as Yogesh and Natasha are there," she said in a matter of fact tone.

"Oh come on, don't drag Natasha into this," I mumbled.

"Why? Because you are in love with her," she shot back on me.

"She is just a good girl and a nice friend." Her straight and blunt statement hurried me into an explanation.

Parvathi rolled her eyes in displeasure, "Don't you fool me. Its written all over your face. A mere mention of her name makes you blush."

She rolled the empty paper cup on the table for a while then looked at me, her lips flickered briefly but then resumed their trademark pout, and I thought she wanted to say something to me but was in doubt.

"Hey angel eyes, you want to say something?" I poked her.

"Mohit, I don't know how you would take it, but I think you should concentrate on your career first. These are early days for you."

For the first time in all those days when we interacted with each other, she grabbed my hand which was on the table. "Natasha is a very ambitious girl, buddy. You might get hurt."

I looked at her wickedly. "Hey Miss Parvathi Thomas, do I smell jealousy?" I wanted to make the moment light.

She withdrew her hand from mine, making a face. "Why should I be jealous? And anyway, I don't believe in all this love shove. To men it's a five minute sex pleasure, but to women it's sacrifice and compromise for life, because children happen as a by-product of that, often accidently. Then men shy away from their responsibilities to rear them and women have to bear all of it for the rest of their lives."

She shocked me again with a strong statement against men. I don't know why she always ended with a bitter note about men, but I wanted to know, once and for all.

"Parvathi, why are you so against the men in the world?" I stopped, waiting for an answer, but she just looked at me and then looked away.

I pleaded after a while, "Hey can you tell me please or I will die guessing what went wrong with you."

She took a deep sigh and almost whispered. "Nothing went wrong with me, but everything went wrong with her."

"Her who?" I asked tilting my head slightly in anticipation of what's to come.

"Rose Thomas, my mother," she said and then went silent.

She picked up her handbag. I thought she was leaving me in the middle of a mystery, so I grabbed her arm.

"Relax! I am not going anywhere, just wanted to have a drag," she said extracting a pack of cigarettes.

This woman sure knew how to create suspense.

I waited patiently as she lighted a cigarette and smoked for a while, blowing thick smoke in the air.

Then she spoke, "You know Mohit, I was to be born as Parvathi Mishra, but I ended up being Parvathi Thomas." I stared at her dumbfounded.

"Do you know why?" she asked. I maintained my silence for I knew that only she had the answer to that question. "Because my father used her, physically, mentally, and left her for dead."

I could sense the anguish in her voice; I kept my silence as she played with her bangles for a while. Strange emotions crossed her face, as if she was living the agony all over again.

I looked at her in anticipation, and wished she would resume her story, but she went into a pause, a dreadful and long pause. I gently placed my hand over hers from across the table. The touch of my hand startled her out of the deep coma. She looked at me, her eyes moist, and her lips trembled.

I could sense that she was in pain, a lot of pain and even though I wanted to hug her, envelope her in my embrace, I patted her hand in consolation instead.

"Leave it Parvathi, let go. I didn't know my questions would bring back painful memories."

She sobbed in response. I gave her a tissue to wipe off tears running down her cheeks, but she sneezed in the tissue instead, rubbed her nose and looked at me innocently.

"Hey, need another coffee?" I asked smiling.

She nodded her agreement.

She wiped off her tears with a tissue, gingerly.

"Now can we have your million-dollar smile back?"

She smiled and mumbled, "Maybe some other time."

"Yeah, may be another time, when you feel completely comfortable to tell me."

(II)

Control, control Mohit control, think about something else, sing a song or sing some bhajan if it helps.

My inner voice, my super ego convinced me to concentrate, to restrain myself from committing something grave, and it wasn't helping much. The Id in me played with my instincts, coaxing me to hold her, grab her and kiss her passionately.

It was the moment which made me realize the virtue of will power. Imagine a situation when you are driving and have a long distance to go and your beloved plays wicked tricks on you. That's what was happening with me.

Natasha had a meeting in Gurgaon and she sought permission from Chinnan to take me along. Needless to say, she got it.

She always had her way with him. Chinnan was too mortal to refuse her. She was a seductress, and only gods could turn her down on a given day.

So, like a love-abiding slave, I drove her car in the midst of heavy morning traffic, a heavy lusty male voice was singing something in English on her music player with an equally seductive background score.

Natasha looked as if she was in a trance; her eyes were closed and she didn't know where her hands were.

Her right hand was somewhere up on my thigh. Or maybe she knew, but didn't care.

Or maybe she didn't know that her hand on my thigh was driving me nuts.

I was like an elephant in rage, full of testosterone, her hand on my thigh sending electric jolts down my spine.

Only if I had been in a jungle, I would have spilled my rage on the trees. But here, in the early morning traffic of Delhi, who cared! Almost everybody is in an overdose of hormones, cussing and abusing each other on their way to the office.

I concentrated on that very seductive, disruptive male voice from the music system to distract myself from the strange ideas that were coming to my head. The display on the music system said that some Chris Issac was singing.

'What a wicked game to play, to make me feel this way.

What a wicked thing to do, to let me dream of you.

What a wicked thing to say, you never felt this way.

What a wicked thing to do, to make me dream of you.'

The more I concentrated on that song, the more I felt like grabbing her.

I had a long way to go, from Okhla to Gurgaon and to keep Natasha safe from my hormonal overdrives, I decided to keep my mind away from those beautiful slender milky white fingers on my thigh and that song.

Even if she was doing this to me on purpose, this wasn't the right time. So I recited multiplication tables from eleven to nineteen, to see if I still remembered the childhood nightmare of mathematics.

She lifted her hand from my lap finally, when we reached the office building of Lovely Cosmetics, a multinational company and one of our key clients.

It took us another fifteen minutes to find a parking space some half a kilometre away from the office building.

A lean man with swollen red eyes took the keys from me as Natasha collected her bearings in a hurry.

Natasha started walking towards the office building in double steps while I took the parking slip from the man.

As I started to move towards her, she almost broke into a trot in a jiffy.

"Natasha, wait, why are you running?" I called from behind.

"Hurry up Mohit, we are late. Can't keep the client waiting," she shouted, gasping for air.

"Come on, be quick, we have to catch a lift to the tenth floor, otherwise that bugger would call up Chinnan that we have not arrived," she half blurted, half gasped as I stepped besides her.

Lovely Cosmetics was a big client and made up nearly the fourth of the monies we earned from the Delhi branch, but the way 'ever so confident, always has her ways' Natasha was desperate to reach on time made me wonder who the person was, whom Natasha fears too.

I had never seen her so shaken, with such a harried look on her face.

I looked around at people on foot, people like us, executives in ties, suits and skirts, all in a hurry. Like puppets attached to a string.

The only exception was the rickshaw puller who basked in the early morning sun with a cup of tea in his hand.

I saw him refusing a passenger, because his need of the hour was tea, not money.

I envied that rikshaw puller, who was sipping his tea with utter pleasure and calm on his face.

No qualms of the past, no worries of the future, no ambition so big to turn you into a slave.

Because he knew he can never be big, his next big ambition would perhaps be to arrange for food in the afternoon. He slurped his tea, smacked his lips and smiled at me. I smiled back, he was living the moment, enjoying every bit of what God had provided him with.

His earnings would be little, but his needs were small too.

He was not a corporate slave like me. He was living on his own terms.

I don't remember clearly when I last had tea in the morning with my bottoms planted firmly on a chair, relaxing. Not since I landed this job.

Every day I prepare tea spinning around to collect my belongings from all over the place, and keep a close eye on two wall clocks with different timings set ahead of the actual time.

Even a five-minute delay on the commode leads me to reach office half an hour late, so have to keep the tummy light in the nights which justifies the cause and effect theory – 'a growling upset tummy' cause can have a 'half day salary cut' effect.

Finally, half-huffing, puffing and panting, we reached the reception of Lovely Cosmetics. A plastic doll-like woman sat behind the reception desk and behind the plastic doll was a wall paper with massive red lips, 'Lovely' written beneath it.

The plastic doll greeted us with a blank look on her face. Natasha enquired about some Ravi Malhotra. The plastic doll opened her lips to speak and I feared the effort might crack the heavy layer of make-up on her face.

Nothing of that sort happened; it was just a figment of my stupid imagination.

Without cracking the make-up on her cheeks, she squeaked that Ravi Malhotra had not arrived yet and we could wait in the meeting room.

Natasha heaved an audible sigh of relief. Her perfect bosom went up and down with the sigh. The plastic doll looked at Natasha with jealousy; I looked at her in awe.

We waited for almost an hour in the waiting room. Natasha killed her time surfing her iPhone and I killed time reading magazines meant for women.

I found the agony aunt column particularly engrossing in one of the magazines and while I was going through the agony of a teenager, who was confused whether he was a male or a female because he felt attracted to both the sexes, the plastic doll came into the cabin and announced that Ravi Malhotra had arrived and would be with us shortly.

Ravi Malhotra did come shortly, actually just as I watched the plastic doll walk away from us across the glass walls of the meeting room. I saw a burly meat ball, rolling and stomping the floor towards us.

"Now here is Ravi Malhotra, Head Marketing Southeast Asia," Natasha said in an undertone, leaving me confused, whether her statement was to warn me, or to remind herself of his stature.

He came in breathing heavily, and with a whistling nose.

Natasha sprang from her seat, almost like a toy doll, and extended her hand for a shake.

"Good Morning Ravi!"

I saw her face as I stood up. She wore her best fake smile reserved for VIP clients, but her eyes were nervous. I was amazed to see that and felt her shaking, but wondered why this meat ball of a man was having such an effect on my ever-so-confident girl.

"Hi Natasha," he grabbed her extended hand but rather than shaking it, he dragged her towards him.

"Sorry mate, I am late, so I am making up with a hug," he said in a heavy, booming voice, as he enveloped her in his heavy, meaty arms.

The slender frame of my lovely lady disappeared in the chunk of cholesterol for a while and I felt a sudden urge of hitting Ravi Malhotra on his bunny face.

"Hmm, you smell so good Natasha, as always," Ravi Malhotra whispered with his eyes closed.

I felt a sudden surge of blood to my temples as I imagined what it would be like if I hit him in the middle of his legs.

She emerged out of his embrace, dizzy and shaken, and it took her some seconds to regain composure.

Now I knew why she was so nervous and insisted that I tag along for this meeting. The meat ball was a pervert.

He settled his chubby behind on a chair in front of us while we reclaimed our empty seats.

Natasha fumbled for her presentation folder, so that she could come straight to business, but Ravi Malhotra was in the mood for small talks.

"You know the road in front of my society is full of sewer water, and that's what made me late today."

"Hmm, it happens," Natasha said in a non-committal tone, as she continued fumbling with her papers.

"Where do you live?" I asked.

He looked at me as if he had discovered an extra button in his trousers.

"I live in a three-crore flat buddy, in the poshest building of Gurgaon." He bragged.

Then he realized that he should have asked why, before bragging about his status.

"But why are you asking?" he asked me.

"And may I know the locality where you live?"

Ravi Malhotra looked at Natasha irritably. Natasha raised her shoulders, and smiled innocently.

She signalled that she had no idea what this was all about.

But Ravi Malhotra answered me nonetheless.

"I live in the best locality of Gurgaon, all the VIPs and corporate giants live there and it is only three kilometres from the highway. In fact, my building is the tallest building in Gurgaon. Natasha, you should visit my home sometime," he said the last line with a slightly swollen chest and lots of pride in his voice.

"And there would be around thirty-five to forty thousand people living in your locality, I presume sir," I continued as Natasha smiled her best fake smile at Ravi Malhotra.

But at the same time, Natasha knocked my leg from underneath the table and the meat ball looked at me with hardened expressions.

"Come to the point brother. I don't have much time to waste," he said in a stern tone.

"Don't take any offence boss, and pardon me, I was only trying to find the solution to your broken road problem."

"And how come," he said sarcastically.

Natasha cleared her throat, rather loudly to indicate that this was it and I have to stop now.

I kept quiet for a moment and Natasha opened her file addressing Ravi Malhotra. "So Ravi ..."

"No no, Natasha, let him complete. Let's see how I can fix my society road," he said in an over smart tone. "So, tell me," Ravi Malhotra looked at me and said in a haughty tone.

"I only just wanted to suggest that since you live in a high-profile society with around 35 to 40 thousand high-profile people, why don't you, I mean why doesn't Lovely Cosmetics take the initiative to build a road to your society?"

"And what will Lovely Cosmetics get out of all this charity?" Ravi Malhotra said sarcastically.

"No boss, it would not be charity at all. You can build the road on the condition that you would maintain the road only if you are given the opportunity to paint the locality red and pink."

Red and pink was the brand color of Lovely Cosmetics.

I continued to explain as I sensed the giant panda had not understood my point clearly.

"See boss, you spend crores on hoardings at prime locations. Imagine painting the back wall of your building with Lovely Cosmetics branding and that too with only having to pay for the maintenance of the road for that branding opportunity."

"And why would I do that? I am not the government. Tomorrow you would say I should build toilets in the villages."

"Why not boss, that's a good idea!"

"Oh, bullshit. Don't try to teach me my job. I have wasted enough of the time on your nonsense," Ravi Malhotra waved his hand in annoyance.

Natasha was waiting for that appropriate moment with the presentation ready on Lovely Cosmetics' new brand launches.

She stepped in quickly and deftly started to brief him about the creative ideas. It took her half an hour to present the same. Ravi Malhotra kept quiet all the while she talked so animatedly.

"So, that's it Ravi. What do you feel about it?" she said after she had summarized.

After a pregnant pause, he opened his mouth.

"Hmm, that's a lovely shade of nail paint babes," he said with a wicked grin on his face.

"Oh! Thanks Ravi," she said with a mock smile. "But it's not from Lovely Cosmetics"

"I know," he said half mockingly but then got serious. "Give me some time. Let me discuss all of the ideas further with our shareholders."

Then he smiled his wicked smile again and said, "Come sometimes without business also, honey."

"Someday Ravi, someday. Bye for now," she said packing her bag quickly, and looked at me briefly.

I understood that it was time to leave.

I was about to leave with her, when Ravi called me.

"Hey social reformer, listen!"

I turned on my foot to face him, "Yeah Ravi."

Natasha peeped from behind my shoulders.

"Not you Natasha. I just want to speak to him for a minute."

"Okay," she said nonchalantly and started walking towards the reception.

He signalled me to close the door.

"Can you pass on a message to Chinnan?"

I nodded in affirmation.

"See, I am in Malaysia for a week in another ten days. Just tell him to arrange for..." he tapped his nose with his finger, "some company."

I was lost for a moment for I was unable to understand what he wanted to imply, and then he tapped his nose again.

"Female company," he said and winked.

I nodded my head in affirmation that I have understood his message and without looking at that filthy man again, I turned around and out of the building, where Natasha was waiting for me.

We covered half of the distance on our way back in profound silence.

Natasha drove the car with a determined pout on her face, negotiating the stubborn traffic. The only noise in the car was of some rubbish RJ on a radio channel, playing fabricated tricks for the audiences.

Then suddenly she looked at me.

"What did that pig say?" she demanded an answer with authority.

"Nothing, he just wanted to speak to Chinnan," I lied.

"That bastard wants to fuck me urgently," she said in response.

Not you, at least for this time, I thought.

"I know why Chinnan sends me to him, on some pretext or the other," she continued.

I knew the answer, but I wanted to know from her, so I asked, "Why?"

"So he can enjoy slithering his filthy hands all over my body and because he hopes someday I would agree to get laid on my own."

I looked at her in shock.

"How can Chinnan think like that! It's so disgusting!" I exclaimed.

"Of course," she looked at me for a brief while, "what's in it for me, only Chinnan would benefit out of this fuck."

We fell into a long silence for a while. I was stunned.

And I was not able to point out a single reason for the dead silence.

Was I stunned to know the thought process of Chinnan or was I stunned to hear what Natasha had said a while earlier.

She spoke again.

"By the way, I liked the way you humiliated that bastard," she said with a sly smile negotiating a turn.

"Like what?"

"Like when you said that," she paused as a biker ahead was determined to come under the wheels of our car.

She braked for half a second, giving vital life to the biker, for which he should have offered some prasad in the mandir, but he didn't know that he had saved his life by a whisker.

That's how fragile life is in Delhi-NCR!

Natasha also didn't realize that she had saved somebody by her presence of mind and continued nonetheless, "Arrey, when you said that he should build the road himself. *Aukat dikha di saale ki.*"

"I never said he should build the road for himself; it should be for the general good. If he would come forward, it would inspire others also to do so in his vicinity."

"Oh, come on! Were you serious?" she made a face.

"Yes I was," I said haughtily.

"You and your ideas," she puffed her hair rounding her lips, giving it an air of 'who cares'.

That's what I liked in her, but she was not her usual self today.

We moved away and ahead of the heavy traffic and my fixation shifted from the road to her face. She knew I was watching her all this while.

She smiled at last with her stare on the road, acknowledging her admirer.

"What were you looking at?" she demanded, as we were just about to enter the parking of our office.

"Lips pouted in concentration, a half-raised brow, some perspiration on the upper lip and a throbbing vein in the neck," I said confidently.

"Hey, you are making me nervous," she blushed as she parked the car in its designated space.

As soon as she parked, I stepped out of the car quickly, and took an opportunity to open the door on her side.

She came out of the car and stretched her limbs out of tiredness, walked two steps towards the stairs and then the inevitable happened. That which I had been avoiding since morning.

The culprit happened to be the pencil heel of her left foot. She lost her balance and was about to dust the floor when I caught her in mid-air.

I grabbed her by the waist and drew her close to me. She found her balance immediately and raised her left leg to look behind at her shoe, to ascertain whether she had a broken heel. This brought her closer to me. I felt her heart beating against mine and her silky hair were in my face.

She removed both of her shoes taking the support of my shoulders and then looked up at me, her full lips inches away from mine. Her eyes seemed indecisive, pleading at me to let her go, but her body still clasped on to me.

I hadn't loosened my grip and she wasn't trying to break free from it.

I drew my face closer to hers. I looked at her perfectly chiselled nose and smelled the aroma of her skin, sensing the pheromones rushing in her.

She closed her eyes as I touched her soft lips with mine, the string of her hair played on my cheeks as our tongues explored each other.

I too closed my eyes, crumbling and reeling under the mellowness of her touch, and then suddenly she went rigid and pushed me away from her.

I let her loose and took two steps back. She looked at the ground and covered her lips with her palm. She then raised her eyes and looked all around in the parking lot, to check if there was anyone else besides us.

I too looked all around to see if anybody was watching us.

Thankfully, there was nobody.

She was already on the foot of the stairs by the time I steadied my wandering gaze back to where she stood.

I called out to her. "Hey Natasha, listen!"

She waved her hand with her back facing me, and continued to climb the stairs. "Not now Mohit, not now and don't come after me, please."

I felt the pleading in her voice and waited in the parking for five minutes before heading to Chinnan's cubicle.

(III)

I saw Chinnan. He was trying to find some hidden treasure trove up his nose with his finger when I reached his cubicle.

Some people stare at ends and some clasp their head with their hands when they are really thinking hard. Chinnan had his own distinct style; he fingered his nose when he ran his brain's horses. So, if Chinnan fingered his nose and fingered it hard, it meant that he was cooking something in his mind.

The finger came out of his nose when he looked at me and for the first time he looked happy to see me in his cubicle.

"Aha, come in Mohit! I was thinking of you," he rubbed his finger on the side of his trousers.

I looked at his finger being sharpened at the side of the trouser and thought, *'So he was thinking of me.'*

"Come, come, have a seat," he pointed at the row of chairs opposite his table.

I was quite surprised as I took a chair, which he had never offered to me in so many months.

I looked at him, and he showed his teeth to me which were cigarette-stained. I had never noticed them, for he had never looked at me and smiled until now.

Either I was in very grave danger or the news of what Ravi Malhotra has said to me had travelled to Chinnan and he was making amends.

I was sure something was fishy.

"Mohit, you know where my house is," Chinnan asked and grinned at me.

"Yes Chinnan," I said wondering whether he really had a lousy memory or he acted like he forgot that I had delivered chicken at his house last Sunday only.

He had an immense faith in me that only I can bring fresh cut chicken for him, and not the delivery boy.

"Here," he handed over the bunch of keys to me. "Take my car. Savita has some important work and I would not be able to go because I have a prescheduled appointment in the evening and may not come home tonight."

I looked at my watch; it was almost 2 p.m.

So ideally, he could have attended to his wife's pressing need if he wanted to.

"And don't tell her that I would not be coming home tonight," he warned me. "Now get going," he waved his hand irritably. Pleasantries over, his work done, he was back to his usual self.

"Chinnan, Ravi Malhotra wanted to pass on a message through me," I said, lifting my bottoms from his visitor's chair.

"I know, I know, he always passes on a message before a major ad campaign," he said irritably. "You get going, otherwise she would call again and eat my head".

I turned and took two steps, when he called me from behind.

"Listen!"

I turned again to face him.

"Just a piece of advice to you. In the real world, you must do anything, just anything, to maintain a client."

He looked at me scornfully and continued, "You can't manage a client with bullshit ideas that you pass on to everybody."

A low whistle came out of my mouth. So Ravi Malhotra had called him after all. I had a hunch that Chinnan had to hunt for that female company tonight.

I wondered how Chinnan managed to foot the bill for these extra services to the client.

Pushing all thoughts aside, I walked towards our work stations.

First and foremost, I had a very important job to do.

I needed to speak to Natasha urgently.

But she was not at her seat.

I dialled her number. It was switched off.

I ran towards the parking, but her car was gone.

The Sin called Mediocrity

(I)

I reached office late the next morning.

I had not slept well – twisted and turned on my bed, thought about that moment, thought of her reaction.

She loved me or she loved me not, that question kept haunting me.

The desire in her eyes showed her love for me, or was it mere attraction? Her sudden dash towards the stairs had expressed her indecision to accept me.

Should I be sorry for what I had done and apologize?

I should say sorry to her first thing in the morning, even though she had also let her guard down.

It was my fault and I should not have taken advantage of her.

My eyes searched for her all over. She was not at her usual place, and she was nowhere as far as my eyes could search.

I asked Yogesh.

"Is Natasha absent today?"

"Who told you?"

Yogesh replied in his usual acid tone.

"I mean, I have not seen her in the office today."

"She went for a client meeting. If you have not noticed, people leave for their field meetings by the time you arrive in the office." He lectured me in his tarty tone.

I turned and walked out of the office, knowing well that there was no point arguing with him over who came to office late more often.

Strolling aimlessly on the streets for a while, I began to feel tired and went to a park nearby.

The park near our office was small but well-maintained. It seemed neglected by the dwellers of Okhla in the morning hours.

I occupied a stone bench in the corner and then looked around. There were a few stray dogs beneath the park benches, and a couple was cozying up under a tree canopy.

Far across at the extreme end of the triangular park. I noticed a familiar silhouette.

She waved at me. It seemed she had already noticed me.

I walked towards her and she beamed a smile at me.

"Are you in a habit of lurking in unusual places at unusual times?" I asked.

"Are you in a habit of finding me there?" she asked.

"Seriously, what are you doing in the park, in the morning?"

"I came here to be alone, away from the mayhem of the office, and also to think of a new punch line for a brand," Parvathi replied patting the bench by her side.

I occupied the space beside her.

She capped her pen and clipped it on the writing pad in her lap.

"So, what are you doing here?" she asked.

I was in no mood to tell her that I had kissed my dream girl yesterday and now I am worried that the dream is about to be shattered.

"I was searching for something to eat, saw the park and came here just to have a look," I said, making up a hasty story.

She looked at me unconvincingly.

"And where were you last evening?"

Now I was also not in the mood to tell her that I had taken Chinnan's wife to the gynaecologist in the evening yesterday, because he was so-called busy.

"Hmm nothing, I went home early yesterday," I lied.

"Don't you think you are acting strange nowadays?" she said in a sharp tone.

I shrugged my shoulders in response.

There was bitter silence for a while.

Her hand dived into the front pocket of her bag and extracted a pack of cigarettes.

I said, "No."

She sighed in response and her hand dived back with the packet in the front pocket.

"Hey listen," she said after a while. "Have you filled up the nomination of 'Best Employee of the Year'?" she asked.

'Best Employee of the Year' was the hot topic of discussion in the office grapevine these days. Everybody wanted to know whether the other was contesting for the prestigious award that the Director announced every year.

There were some people who thought that they had done something special this year and everyone amongst them was a self-proclaimed hero, saviour of the agency, without whom the agency could not have survived another year.

But nobody wanted to divulge to the other as to what he or she had done in order to achieve the award.

Then there were some whose sole purpose was to create speculation.

I was told by one of the speculators that 'Best Employee of the Year' award kick-started the appraisal and the employee evaluation process. It is that phase of the year when the best of friends became foes.

The award was special because it guaranteed instant recognition, double promotion, a handsome salary hike and a fully sponsored, all expense paid foreign trip. But it was tough... tough because the contestant had to prove how he or she had affected the company's business radically. To top it all, there was no guarantee that the management would give the award to anybody at all.

There had been years when the award wasn't given to anybody.

I had not filled up the nomination form. It was not on my priority list and I sincerely believed I was not worth it.

"No, I have not," I said.

"Why?" Parvathi gave me a surprised look.

"Because I don't think I deserve it. People handle big clients, big businesses here," I said picking a pebble from the ground.

"I handle small, local clients," I said testing my arm strength as I tossed the pebble high up in the air.

"Hmm," she murmured thoughtfully.

I walked back to the office, leaving her behind.

I entered the office and saw Natasha walking towards me, in the corridor.

Her eyes were glued on the phone, that's why perhaps she had not noticed me at once.

I inched closer to her, mentally preparing myself to face her.

I covered the distance almost in stealth mode, planting feet firmly on the ground, as if to catch a butterfly in the garden, because I was afraid that my butterfly would fly away upon seeing me.

My stealth failed in front of the woman's sixth sense. Natasha raised her head, just when I was at an arm's length from her.

She looked at me, first with no expression on her face, as if trying to recognize me, and then she arched her brows, turned sharply and in quick steps started walking in the opposite direction.

"Hey Natasha, listen!" I called after her.

She paid no heed to my call and continued with her quick pace.

I called her again, but to no avail.

She reached the glass door which separated the corridor from the workstations.

I was fast losing the opportunity to speak to her in isolation

"Hey Barbie, please listen," I called after her, almost pleading.

This time calling her worked like Eno against acidity.

She turned quickly and stormed towards me like a fire engine.

I thought she was charging in to push me or slap me, but she stopped centimetres away from my nose.

"Who told you my pet name?" she demanded with blaring eyes.

I smiled wickedly, teasing her.

She continued locking her eyes with mine for a while.

"Don't you dare call me by that name in office again," she chewed every word when she realized that I wasn't going to tell her how I knew her pet name.

"You were not listening and I wanted to say sorry," I said.

She folded her arms, still looking at me angrily.

Now that was an opportune time for apologies.

I clasped my ears and imitated a baby's voice.

"Sorry miss, it would not happen again."

Her stance softened a bit and I saw a small encouraging smile playing on her lips, which she tried hard to suppress.

"Can we be friends?" I asked with all the innocence of a child, still clasping my ears.

"Ohoo, stop this drama, somebody would see," she said irritably.

"Can we be friends?" I asked in my usual baritone voice this time.

"Promise me that you would not gossip about what happened in the basement parking with anybody," she asked.

"I promise."

"Promise me that it will not happen again."

"I promise, not without your permission."

"Promise me that you would not try to act smart, like you are trying to act just now," she said with utmost seriousness as she started walking in the corridor.

"Promise me that you would only speak to me when I permit you to," she continued.

"Now this is tyranny," I complained.

"Then I am sorry, you cannot be my friend," she said flatly.

"Ok, ok," I surrendered.

"Do you want to accompany me to the ladies' room," she asked suddenly pointing at a door in front of her.

"No no, take your time." I had followed her unconsciously, and had landed right in front of the ladies' washroom.

"So, are we friends now?" I asked desperately as she was about to disappear behind the door.

"Do you want me to write it on a stamp paper?" I heard her voice from behind the door.

I heaved a sigh of relief and returned to my workstation.

'Best Employee of the Year' nomination form was lying right in front of my eyes on the table.

Somebody had taken a printout and kept it on my table.

I smiled. None other than Parvathi would have done that.

I picked it up, read it and re-read it.

Then I called up each one of my clients one by one and requested them for one thing.

And fortunately, each one of them agreed on that thing.

By the end of the day, a bunch of appreciation letters were on my table, each one personally signed by the client and addressed to the Director.

I took the nomination form home that evening.

It took me three hours to fill it with satisfaction.

I sealed it in the envelope and with a thick blue pen labelled the envelope 'Private and Confidential'.

The next morning, I posted the envelope to the Director's office.

(II)

Two months passed quickly. Those who had drawn swords during the appraisal period had become friends again, at least on the outside.

We were moving towards the end of the year and the agency was running on all engines, with a hectic pace to maintain deadlines for several clients.

The buzz around the 'Employee of the Year' award died, partly due to busy schedules of the employees and partly because the period of one or two months after appraisals was considered crucial. Every employee feared that he or she was under observation by the management.

The management knew this fact very well and used this fear of the employees to exert pressure and extract more work out of their misery.

I wasn't very worried about the prying eyes of the management though. I was more worried about Natasha's change in attitude towards me.

I thought she would become her usual self with me after our patch-up and I would graduate from being 'just friends' to a higher one eventually, but she had kept her word.

I didn't know she was serious when she literally instructed me that I could only speak to her when she wanted me to.

She was her normal self in the office. We still discussed work, though I felt that she wasn't much interested now in what I was doing.

She still smiled at me, but the smile had no warmth. It was more her smiling at the pizza guy while taking the box of pizza over the counter – cursory and formal.

There were times when I stepped into the office and found her laughing heartily on some joke cracked by Yogesh, but as soon as she noticed that I had arrived, she would stop immediately and go back to work, as if she did not want to encourage me to be party to her happiness.

Desperation was settling in once again. I wanted to express my feelings for her once and for all. I wanted her to decide on my fate. I wanted her to answer – 'yes' or 'no'. I wanted to move on from the dilemma, the state of limbo, for I had wasted enough time plucking the flower petals chanting 'she loves me, she loves me not'.

But I needed a change in the setting, a change in the mood and the atmosphere to do so.

The change in the mood and the setting came just when I had made up my mind to ask her out on a coffee date.

The Director announced a party on the coming weekend.

His mail said that each one of us had performed well and the agency had registered good profits owing to all the hard work, so it was time to celebrate the success and to announce the much awaited-awards and rewards.

The party would be an appropriate opportunity to draw Natasha's attention, I was sure. Maybe to find a lonely corner and express my feelings towards her. I started counting days to the weekend.

With still three days to go, the mood in the agency changed to that of festivities.

(III)

"Hey, come through the staff door next time."

A handsome man on the duty manager's desk advised me in a stern, authoritative tone as I entered the lobby of the hotel.

"Pardon," I said, surprised by the way he had spoken to me.

"And where is your bow tie?" he said coming towards me.

"Bow tie?" I was utterly confused. Was there some kind of dress code to the party that I was not aware of.

"Is there some dress code to the party?" I asked him.

It was his turn to look confused now.

"Are you not the new joinee?"

Did I look like a new joinee to him?

"I am here to attend the party hosted by AAA Advertising."

I took out the printed guest list and showed that to him.

His stance softened immediately.

"Sorry sir, I apologize for my mistake," he pleaded.

"It's ok," I said.

"Come sir, I will show you to the party area."

I followed him and as soon as I reached the venue of the party and looked at the service staff, my heart sank. I immediately realized why the duty manager had confused me for a new joinee.

It was a dressing disaster, a blunder. I had dug out a nice blue formal jacket from Sameer's wardrobe and wore the same with black trousers and white shirt. It looked suave on me, but not so suave on the serving staff of the resort.

The only difference between my attire and their uniform was the bow tie. The irony of the situation was that I couldn't even turn back and go for a change because the resort was some forty odd kilometers away from my house. Add to it that I had express instructions from Chinnan that I had to be at least two hours early to the venue, so I could supervise the arrangements, guest list and stuff.

In others words, it was a party for 150 odd employees of the agency, but I was still on duty, overseeing who was downing how many pegs of whisky.

After an hour of supervising the branding of venue with cut-outs designed especially for the party, I waited patiently, with two hostesses at the welcome gate.

I had a very important job to do. I had to place a tick mark against names of guests as and when they arrived. Important job indeed, if one had to keep a tab on the party bill, and I was the chosen one to keep count of the plates and the pegs.

Our agency's administrative department had to do the job, but being the all-women department, they were short on men above the level of peon, and the two ladies of the admin department were in no mood to sacrifice their make-up and dressing time.

So Chinnan became their hero, saviour of the damsels in distress because he suggested that he can deploy one guy who is above the level of peon. Then what? I was sacrificed in the name of mascara and foundation.

After half an hour of waiting, the first one to arrive was Sardar Harpal Khanna of the Avengers group.

He was famous as a strict disciplinarian, a teetotaler and a fitness freak. I didn't have to ask his name for he was also famous for his off-the-lid temperament and that was the only reason he had arrived without any company.

One of the girls handed him a rose bud as I ticked off his name from the sheet.

Then one by one, people started flocking the venue.

Some acknowledged me as one of them, some just didn't care.

Natasha came with Chinnan and Yogesh.

My god! It was so hard to tear my eyes away from her.

She looked so astounding and an ultimate diva in the off-shoulder short black dress.

"Good!" Chinnan exclaimed patting my back as I ticked off their names from the list.

Parvathi came alone, as expected, and was the only one dressed in the casual tee and jeans with her hair tied up in her signature bun. It looked like she had come straight from the office and hadn't had the time for a change of clothes.

But then she was like that only. Carefree.

I ticked her name off, as she made a face looking at me and my dress.

I shooed her away with a hand signal as I spotted the Director coming behind her.

He went past us like a breeze, without even bothering to flash an eyelid on minnows.

After about an hour outside at the entrance, I entered the lounge and walked to the bar counter.

I ordered a whisky and sipped on it, taking in the scene in front of me.

The party was getting hotter by the moment. The younger lot of the agency were shaking their booty on Mick Jagger and the older lot had occupied the round tables around the dance floor.

The older lots were enjoying their roast and drinks, all the while ogling at beauties around them.

My eyes wandered off to the far side of the lounge where the Director was with his gang of loyalists. They were lined up to have a drink and a few words with him.

He waved some of them off with a brush of his hand, as if shooing mosquitoes away from his ears. He had a bored look on his face.

The scene reminded me of Don Corleone in *The Godfather*.

Then my eyes wandered off to another far corner where a lone figure sipped on some orange drink with an equally bored look on her face.

I walked slowly towards her; avoiding the gang of heavily drunk couples throwing every bit of their moving body parts in the air.

I pulled a chair beside her, she acknowledged me with a smile.

Conversations were difficult with the background of loud music, so we both ended up looking at the dance floor.

The track changed from a peppy number to a sensuous one. I spotted Natasha dancing with Yogesh.

Her flawless moves could have turned on even the noblest saint on the planet.

It appeared that she was drunk... drunk and happy. They both were dancing so provocatively, that at times, not even a wisp of air could have passed from between their bodies.

Suddenly the whisky started to taste bitter.

"Why are you not dancing?" Parvathi whispered in my ear.

"I am not the dancing types," I replied, trying unsuccessfully to tear my eyes off Natasha.

"Me too." She replied patting my hand in consolation, as if she knew where it was hitting me.

Suddenly Natasha broke off from Yogesh and half-dancing, half-walking tipsily, went straight to the Director's table and dragged him for a dance.

He came to the dance floor with her like a lamb that needed a shepherd.

They started dancing and almost immediately people on the dance floor stopped dancing, making a semi-circle around Natasha and the Director.

After about five minutes of solo dancing, the girls on the dance floor joined in to share the Director with Natasha, as their male partners looked on, dumbfounded.

Another five minutes later, the Director decided that he had had enough of being the Kanha of the Gopis and signalled at the DJ to stop the music.

He asked for a mike after that.

The hostess handed him one almost immediately. He tapped his finger on the mouth piece to check if it was working.

The party, which was bustling with music a while ago, now went silent, for people who were going gaga over each other were now high with anticipation. The moment had arrived... the moment for announcements.

The Director whistled slowly in the mouth piece, appreciating the pin drop silence.

His 'hello my dear friends' was greeted with a strong applause.

"This year was a great year for us. We had great business, and we made good profits. This could not have happened without the support of each one of you."

Then he took a pause, looking into the eyes of people circling him.

There was a slow-measured applause this time.

He continued to speak as the applause died.

"You all work for a big international agency with big international clients and you fight each day to maintain these clients, meet their deadlines, but..."

He stopped his sentence mid-way, which added some more drama and suspense to the scene.

"But, my dear friends, one thing happened for the first time in Delhi and that thing has created a benchmark for other branches, all over India." There was pin-drop silence now.

"Do you know what that one thing is?" he asked a girl from the Avengers group, who had been rubbing her behind at his groin provocatively while dancing.

She shook her head in the negative, with her wide-astonished eyes fixed on the Director.

He shook his head in pity, as if he had expected a better response from the girl, but then continued to speak.

"My dear ones, for the first time in the history of the agency, Delhi branch met all its expenses on its own, and even made profit." Then he made a pinch of salt gesture with his fingers and added, "however small."

He again looked at the curious faces around him.

Faces who had circled him and tried to grab his attention when he was having his drinks, now looked confused, which indicated to him that people had not understood the statement.

"Meeting the expenses on its own means that even if I take away all the international and national clients given to us by our head office, I am still in profits."

The confusion was replaced by awe on some of the faces. "Do you know why?"

He looked at the circle around him.

People were surrounding the Director, in the order of influence and weightage of a person in the agency.

I was in the outer third circle. The last one.

I thought the Director had raised the genuine question, just to check the IQ of the audience, and I half-raised my hand only to realize that the Director wasn't in the mood to quiz. He was going gung-ho and was rather enjoying the moment.

He had asked the question just to add some spice and to ridicule.

So, he continued nonetheless, without waiting for anyone to answer.

"Because apart from the big businesses, we paid attention to the small businesses also. We added small local clients to our portfolio, which had never happened earlier."

Parvathi, who stood next to me, squeezed my hand in reaction to the Director's statement.

"There are some people in our agency who strived hard to win these local clients for us. Especially one of them has been exceptional in this task, I must say," he continued.

Some people in the third and second circle and even few from the first stole quick glances at me.

I squeezed Parvathi's hand this time, feeling proud and re-assured that my hard work had finally paid off and the management had acknowledged it.

The Director took a few steps towards Chinnan and patted his shoulder with a heavy hand. "I congratulate Chinnan and his Star Wars team for achieving this feat."

Chinnan obliged him with his trademark gargling sound that he emitted from his mouth when feeling happy.

"And now for the biggest question of the evening," the Director raised his voice and clapped his hands twice as if to gather the attention of one and all present.

"Who would get the 'Employee of the Year' award?"

He paused for a moment, as if we all knew the answer and weren't telling him all the while.

"Believe me, my friends, there were a lot of nominations from all branches across India and I feel proud that the 'Employee of the Year' award goes to an employee of the Delhi branch."

He took a swig at his Scotch that had been resting on the small table right next to him and continued taking too much time to announce the name.

I took my handkerchief out to wipe off the sweat from my palms.

"Official communication would follow, but I would announce the name here anyway."

He paused again, looking at the people around him, to gauge the impact of his words.

"I would like to tell you the achievements of this employee. This employee brought fifteen new clients to the agency, which makes more than one client in a month. How remarkable is that!"

Parvathi nudged me with her elbow and whispered in my ear, "Go, go forward! He is about to announce your name."

The Director again took a short break for he emptied his glass of Scotch in one go this time and signalled the bar girl for a refill.

I started to move slowly around the semi-circle, to reach near the Director as he would announce my name.

"And the employee of the year award goes to Miss Natasha Anand."

Stunned, I stopped a few paces away from the Director, as Natasha clasped her mouth with her hands, faking a shock.

Although it was debatable as to who was more shocked, me or her.

I could not believe my ears. Had I heard the name wrong?

How was this possible? Fifteen clients, exactly what I had written in my nomination form – real estate companies, educational institutes, hosiery, they were the hard-earned clients and I had sweated for the whole year to win them, to maintain them.

And it was all gone in a second?

Was my nomination form lost somewhere?

"Congratulations to Natashaaaaa!"

In the meantime, everybody congratulated Natasha in chorus and she beamed like a rock star, enjoying her new-found fame.

She blew kisses in the air, as the Director patted her back.

Chinnan clapped and Yogesh scooped her from the floor in excitement.

With strange feelings, a mix of disappointment, pain and dejection, I turned back from the scene and walked slowly towards the washroom.

Parvathi walked towards me with a worried look on her face, but I gestured at her to stay where she was.

I didn't need anybody or any consolation.

I just wanted to be alone.

I felt like crying.

I wanted to be away from these people. I wanted to go home. I wanted to go to my small town where people were simple... maybe less ambitious, but happier.

I wept silently behind the closed doors of the lavatory.

I was hurt, not because I didn't get the award which was rightfully mine.

I felt hurt because I was cheated on.

I didn't know how, but I was cheated on by the same girl whom I had loved so much.

I don't know for how long I sat on the commode, weeping like a lost soul.

When the tears dried, I came out of the lavatory, washed my face, and then checked the pockets of my trousers to check if my bike keys were still with me.

There was no use going back to the party hall. A faint sound of the music was still audible from the closed doors of the venue, but the sound which was music to my ears a while ago felt like hot lava now.

Strange how your state of mind changes the way you see things around you.

I walked towards the basement.

My bike was parked at the far end in the basement and with heavy legs and leaden heart, I walked between the rows of pillars.

I heard a girl's giggle and some whispers from behind a pillar.

I stopped immediately because I knew who giggled like this when happy.

I slowly and silently walked towards the pillar and peered cautiously behind it.

Natasha and Yogesh were leaning on a car with drinks in their hands.

They were speaking in a low voice but were audible from where I was hiding.

"At times I thought you were seriously falling in love with him," Yogesh said.

"With him, seriously?" Natasha said laughing, faking a surprise. "That villager?"

She laughed hysterically for a while, as if she was in fits, then she composed herself and did her trademark jig, blowing her hairs with an 'o' of her lips.

"Not even on my bad days."

Then she tilted her head to one side. The way she would do when she wanted to fake sincerity.

"He was head-over-heels in love with me from day one, so it was as easy as a snap of a finger. One smile, one kiss and he was all mine." I couldn't believe what I was hearing.

"He can walk on his nose for me," she said boasting, "but it's no fun. The real fun is in snatching from under the nose."

"I hope you never went further than the kiss," Yogesh said in his trademark 'death in the house' tone.

"Oh come on! I am ambitious, but no fool," she replied in an equally serious tone, then wrapped her hands on his neck saying lightly, "Janeman, I know who deserves my fuck and whom I can manage with only a kiss."

They took the sips of their drinks in silence for a while, then suddenly Natasha giggled in stupor.

"Poor fellow, he would be wondering what hit him?"

"Poor fellow?" Yogesh reacted with a distorted face and clear hatred in his voice.

"So you would have liked that," he said poking his finger in the air, "that fellow from a third grade institute of god knows which small town would have had walked away with that award. We, pass-outs from top colleges of India, would have slogged while he would have climbed the corporate ladder?" He emphasized on we with a finger on Natasha's chest.

"Never, never!" Natasha said in drunken determination.

I ducked behind a car as they started moving towards the lift.

I saw Yogesh slipping his hand on her waist tightly as they walked.

I had been disappointed earlier, but now I was stumped, and very angry.

All those moments that I had spent with Natasha kept playing in my mind on a loop.

How could I forget walking down the street aimlessly hand in hand with her or dancing with her in the night clubs?

I recalled how she had buried her face in my chest while watching a horror movie. How could I forget conversations with her when she always sounded so concerned whether I had had my dinner.

Was all that just drama?

And for what purpose, why had she staged all of this?

She could have asked me, ordered me that she needed my achievements and I would have happily given her the credit for all that I have done.

I was so much in love with her, she just needed to ask. But she wanted to snatch, I guess. For fun!

Was I just a muse for her, a play thing?

So, that was the real face of Natasha, the ambitious bitch who feigned love to me and ruined me emotionally.

But why me. I wasn't asking anything from them, I was just doing my job.

Yes, I was in love, one-sided love, an admiration or infatuation until she came to me and responded with love, a fake love.

I was also ambitious, everybody is ambitious but I wasn't stomping on somebody's emotion as she did.

Oh, how much I was in love with this girl?

There was only one thing in my mind now.

Why did you do this to me Natasha? Why me?

Is it a sin to fall in love with an ambitious girl, or is it a sin to be from a humble background? Is it a sin to be from a mediocre college or is it a sin to be from a small town? Is mediocrity really a sin?

Wrestling with the Pig

(I)

"Mohiiiit... Mohhhiiiittt."

A woman called me. The voice sounded in pain, the woman was in distress and needed help.

But it was pitch dark. My ears searched for the source of the cry.

My ears were pinned to the cry of the woman and my eyes were trying to adjust to the darkness.

Where exactly was I?

I closed my eyes, so that my eyes could adjust to the darkness.

Then I opened them slowly.

I was standing by a bench in a park and it was still dark and I could barely see beyond my arm's length.

The woman gave an agonizing shrill cry again.

I decided to walk towards the cry relying on my ears and took cautious baby steps towards the source of the voice.

The cry of the woman was getting clearer and so was my understanding of the surroundings, as I moved towards the faint glimmer of light.

After a while, I entered a building compound which looked abandoned, yet very familiar to me.

I tried to figure out where I had seen the heavy carved door to the entrance of the building, and then I saw the poster of a superhero endorsing a famous underwear brand.

Oh, how could I forget that comical poster. I was in fact in my office compound.

But why did it look abandoned?

The cry of the woman was deafening now and was coming from inside the office building.

I gave a push to the door and it gave way. I stepped inside, anticipating that the guard would be stationed behind the desk as usual, but there was nobody. No guard and no desk. In fact, no glass door behind which were the labyrinth of workstations.

I was standing at the entrance of yet another compound, it seemed. There were no rooms, no corridors, no workstations, no people, nothing... just plain ground covered with walls.

There was bright illumination in the middle of the ground as if somebody had focussed light on something round and stony.

Then the shrill cry for help came again and this time I was sure that it had come from inside that round, stony thing.

I took quick steps towards it and as I moved forward, it became clear that it was a water well.

Now that was strange and hilarious. From where on the earth did that water well come into my office building? It seemed I had never been to that part of the office.

"Mohittt," the woman called me again. I reached the boundary wall of the well and peeped inside.

There was indeed a woman inside the well, stark naked, head in the knees, bundled up like a foetus, sobbing incoherently.

I looked at the figure in the well, my shadow looming large over her.

My throat was dry, and tongue seemed to be tied in a knot as no words came out.

I had no idea how this woman landed in the well.

I shouted, "Hey, are you okay?"

The woman raised her head slowly, giving me the horror of my life.

A chill ran down my spine and a sharp cry escaped my mouth. I recognized the woman in distress.

"Natasha!"

She looked at me with big sad eyes, sobbing, weeping and cried for help raising her arms. "Please help me, Mohit."

I reached for the rope nearby but the wicked me reasoned.

Why help her after what she did to you Mohit? Let her rot in hell, she deserved this treatment. God has punished her for all the wrong she has done to you.

I looked at her again, still unsure, with the rope in my hand.

She had hope written all over her face. She wiped her tears off with the back of her hand, looking at me.

Another wrong cannot make right all the wrongs she had done, the human in me reasoned. You loved her and you still love her. God has sent you to save her, not to punish her.

I undid my shirt and threw it towards her so she could cover herself.

Then I lowered the rope in the well, holding it tightly. She caught hold of it and with extraordinary agility and super human strength climbed back to the mouth of the well.

I gave her my hand, to support her.

She caught me by the elbow.

Then her expressions changed. She gave me a wicked grin and her eyes turned witchy.

She gave me a jerk.

I lost my balance.

And the situation turned in a flick of a second.

She was out of the well and I was holding on to her hand.

I looked at her in disbelief.

"Natasha! No," was all that I could utter, because she left my hand.

It was the moment when she was laughing at me, and I was falling in the darkness, when I heard my name being called, "Mohiiit."

I was strewn on the floor, hurt and wounded but somebody was still calling me.

Then I heard the knock, and the call of my name again.

Then I heard the faint sound of the chimes.

Was that my doorbell?

Suddenly the brick walls of the well turned into a wall painted white.

I fluttered my eyes and looked at the wall opposite my cot.

I was dreaming after all. A very bad dream indeed.

That witchy bitch wasn't leaving me alone even in my dreams.

Then I heard the doorbell again.

There indeed was somebody at the door, adamant to wake me up from my deep slumber.

I heard a commotion outside the main door, and then the doorbell rang again, and a woman called my name.

I tried to get up from the cot. I felt tired and weak, as if somebody had sapped the energy out of me.

After two unsuccessful attempts, I planted my feet on the floor and with wobbly legs, moved towards the main door.

I opened the door and saw Parvathi and the next-door neighbour Mr Khanna.

Seeing me at the door, she gave a sigh of relief at first, then asked harshly, "Why are you not coming to the office these days?"

I gave her a faint smile

"It's been three days since anyone saw you or heard from you," she said. "You know how worried I was!"

I looked tiredly at Khanna, our non-existent but present next-door neighbour, who liked to peep out rather than speak-out of his front door.

Khanna mumbled some excuse to me and went his way.

Pulling Khanna out of his door would have been a herculean task for this girl, I thought.

"Can I at least come in?" she demanded.

"Oh sorry," I mumbled and stepped aside to give her way.

I turned and at that moment my feet touched something round and slippery and I lost my balance.

In a split second, I was on the floor, spread-eagled, face up and with butterflies in my eyes.

My head had hit the floor, and the culprit, the empty bottle of Rum was lying by my side.

"Oh my god!" she exclaimed rushing in, throwing her handbag on the floor.

She supported me from behind as I tried to stand up from the floor.

Slowly, she walked me to the bed, then grasped me by the elbow as I tried to sit up on the bed.

"Oh Jesus!" She touched my forehead, "You have high fever."

"Mhmm..." was all that I could mumble with whatever little energy I had remaining.

She looked around and saw four or five empty bottles of liquor on the floor.

Then she looked at me with surprise

"Good lord, what have you done to yourself?"

I shrugged my shoulder in response.

She looked at me disapprovingly for a while, then ordered.

"Just lie down."

I gave her a shy guilty smile.

"Where is your friend?" she asked.

"London." I gasped.

"Have you eaten anything in the past few days or were you happy being Devdas?" she asked as she collected the empty bottles from the floor.

She looked at me for a moment, as if half expecting me to answer, but I was too tired to even utter a word, let alone a sentence, so I kept mum.

I had had something, as I remembered opening two or three packs of peanuts a few days ago, but that was hardly worth mentioning to her.

"Ok, I am going out. I will be back in couple of hours. I hope you will survive by then," she said scorning. "After all, you have survived three days like this."

She turned to walk out of the flat, took a few steps towards the door, and then turned to face me again. "Please try not to close the door from the inside," she said in a polite tone this time. "I will lock it from outside, okay?"

I mumbled, a faint "Okay."

My eyes followed her to the door as she walked out, locking the door from the outside. I kept staring at the door for some time in anticipation, then I dozed off.

I don't know for how many hours I slept. I came back to my senses when I heard some commotion at the door, then the sound of the keys turning the lock.

She entered with a jute bag in her hands and a man tailing behind her.

"Here is your patient doctor," she said pointing at me, as if I wasn't a patient but a sinner waiting for my judgment.

"I don't need...," I tried to resist being examined by a doctor.

"Shhhh," she hushed me, keeping a finger on her mouth, and glared at me with her big black eyes.

I fell silent like an obedient child.

The doctor checked me thoroughly, while she kept looking at me critically with her arms folded on her chest.

The doctor removed his stethoscope, took a deep sigh and turned towards her.

"I don't think there is anything wrong with him," he said.

I gave a sly smile to her, indicating that I already knew it and she had just wasted her time and money on the doctor.

"But he has fever and is very weak and I think it is stress and anxiety that's eating him," he said, speaking to no one in particular. With that, he pulled out his writing pad from his briefcase.

"He should take rest for two to three days," he said jotting some medicines on the paper.

The doctor handed over the prescription to her; she thanked him and looked at me with 'now you know' smile.

Then she walked out with the doctor, locking the front door behind her again.

I stared at the jute bag which she had left on the table.

She came back with some vegetables and fruits this time. Casting a fleeting look at me, she went straight to the kitchen. I heard her fumbling with the utensils.

She came back to the table tying her hair in a bun high up on her head.

With a busy look on her face, she unzipped the jute bag and fished out the first item, a cardinal pack of cigarettes, then some clothes and a towel.

She grabbed the clothes and went out of my eye scope, to the bathroom.

I closed my eyes, feeling dizzy with the much labourious task of watching her dancing around the apartment.

Then I heard the whistle of the pressure cooker, which finally got some work to do after years of lying idle in the cabinet, then the hissing sound of the shower falling on the floor.

Suddenly the apartment felt alive.

I felt an unexplained sense of calm and peace from the medley of the pressure cooker and the shower and drifted into sleep.

I felt a cold hand on my forehead. I turned in the bed.

Parvathi was leaning over me, looking at me with concern.

"Can you sit by yourself?" She asked.

I nodded. "Yes, I can."

She grabbed me by the arms as I tried to get up and acquire a sitting position on the bed.

She was so close to me that I could smell fresh lavender on her skin.

"I have prepared some porridge for you because you have to eat something, then you can take the medicine." She picked up a bowl from the table.

"It's not too hot or too cold," she said handing over the bowl to me. "Eat!"

I took the bowl from her obediently and ate it slowly while she watched me with rapt concentration, as if I would disappear.

When I had finished the porridge, she handed me a glass of water with some pills. I gulped all of it.

I felt some strength coming in me.

"Why are you doing all this?" I said in a tired tone.

"Because we are friends," she said with warmth in her eyes, "and a good friend never leaves the other in distress."

She took the empty bowl from my hand and gave me the thermometer.

"Why did she do that to me? I loved her, but she was not in love with me. She used me," I said in a tired voice.

"I tried to warn you a lot of times, but you were blind in your love for her," she said looking at her fingers

"I told you, love is such a waste of time. Nowadays, everybody in love has a selfish motive," she checked the temperature gauge in the thermometer. "When the motive is gone, love is also gone."

I sighed. Maybe she was right after all.

"Hmm, you still have high temperature," she said adjusting her reading glasses on the bridge of her nose.

The way she looked out of her glasses brought a faint smile on my face. It was so funny and amusing, a girl in her late twenties, peering out of her reading glasses.

She saw me smiling stupidly at her.

"What's so funny, big boy?" she said smiling back at me.

"Nothing," I said with a sobre face this time.

"Then take some rest. I have some cleaning to do in the kitchen"

I checked my watch for the first time and looked at Parvathi with surprise.

"It's ten in the night. Aren't you going home?"

"No," I heard her voice.

She was already on her way to the kitchen.

"Don't you get worried about what people would say, you staying with me overnight?" I asked.

"I give a shit and I care a damn of what people say anyway," she answered without looking back at me. "Besides, who has the time here to look what's happening next door?"

I nodded mentally to that. She was right yet again. Nobody really cared.

(II)

I woke up to a beautiful morning the next day, a bright and sunny day and I could smell the fresh morning air mixed with a whiff of omelette.

I was feeling much better than the previous day, although I was still weak and had a numb feeling in the body. Planting my feet on the floor, with some effort, I walked towards the kitchen.

I looked around the apartment. It was so neat and clean; everything was arranged on to a tidy place, apartment windows were open for a change, because neither Sameer nor I ever had a chance to open the windows of the apartment and let the fresh air in.

All the non-living inhabitants of our apartment, beanbags, book rack, plastic chairs, etc., looked so new and fresh. It seemed like I wasn't in my own apartment but was a visitor to someone else's apartment.

Parvathi stood bare feet in the speckless neat kitchen, donning pink shorts and a sleeveless tee.

A strain of hair on her forehead was in a mood to disturb her in her chores.

She wiped the beads of perspiration off her upper lip, tossing the egg batter in the frying pan.

Then she noticed the movement at the door and looked towards me.

"Hi! Good morning. How are we doing today?" she beamed.

"I am better today," I said leaning on the door ledge. "I never knew that the tiles of the kitchen were blue, I always thought they were grey."

She only smiled to the compliment, too busy switching sides of the omelette.

I heaved a deep sigh. How had I imagined Natasha doing what now Parvathi was doing in the kitchen!

What a fool I had been.

"Hey, will you freshen up? Breakfast is almost ready," Parvathi said, breaking my daydream.

"Aye aye, ma'am," I said dramatically, bowing my head in front of her.

She laughed to that, with lots of warmth in her eyes.

"So, would you join office tomorrow?" she asked me when I came back to the breakfast table.

"I don't know," I said picking up the cup of tea.

"What do you mean don't know?" she said in a bossy tone.

I kept chewing the breakfast, unable to explain to her that I had lost motivation and interest to continue with the job. I didn't want to feel awkward with Natasha around in the office.

"Don't give me that look, Mohit," she warned looking at the expressions on my face.

"I would resign," I said finally when she continued staring at me.

"Are you a fool?" she snapped. "Just because some girl used you for her benefit, you would leave the job without finding another one?"

I stayed mum, more lost in my thoughts than her concern. "And what would you do after that?" she lectured. "Go back to Sirsaganj, haan?"

I nodded, yes, I would go back to Sirsaganj. At least people there were not double-faced.

"And what about the loans that you have taken for your house and little brother's education?" she reasoned.

"So, you tell me what I should do?" I said in a frustrated tone. "I don't want to see her face. After whatever I heard that night, I know I can't."

"She should be ashamed of what she had done, not you," she argued. Then, she joined her hands, as if pleading, and continued, "and please for god's sake, I don't want another Rose Thomas in the making."

"What happened to her Parvathi, you never told me?"

"I will tell you because you are going in that direction. You will end up ruining everything like my mother, because of the filthy feeling called love," she said scornfully.

"Oh come on Parvathi! Give her some respect, she is your mother," I said politely.

"I don't know Mohit. I really don't know how a mother should be like."

"Why?"

"Because I have always seen her in the mental asylum," she said in a broken voice.

"What?" was all that I could utter.

"Yes, I grew up in an asylum for mentally challenged. nurses there literally adopted me, taking care of my mother and my education," she took a break to take a swig from her tea. "When I grew up, I asked them, how my mother landed in that place and I gathered information from the nurses and acquaintances of my mother."

She sighed deeply, as if to contemplate whether to go ahead with her narrative or not, but continued, "When my mother first came to the asylum, she was seven months pregnant, unable to tell who the father of her unborn child was because she had lost her nerves."

"So what happened with her?" I asked curiously.

"Love happened," she smiled scornfully. "I went to my granny in Bihar and convinced her to narrate the story of my mother. She told me that my mother was a brilliant student and a haughty girl. Much against the wishes of her father, she came to Delhi to become an IAS officer."

Parvathi looked beyond me at the wall, as if I was not there at all.

"My nana was a poor man; he could not have afforded her living in Delhi. So she started giving tuition to other IAS aspirants at a coaching center.

One of her students was my father, and they would study together even after regular tuitions. Gradually my mother started developing a soft corner for him. They moved in together, partly because they wanted to save the cost of living, and partly because they had a single motive – to crack the IAS examination. Not just that, majorly, they both had started to love each other. It was a bold decision because although they were both from Bihar, one was a Christian and the other a Brahmin."

She fell silent again, and I prompted her to go on. "Then?"

"Then they both cleared the prelims and started concentrating on the mains. That's when my mother started losing interest in her own studies and started concentrating on my father's."

"Why?" I asked.

"Because they had been playing with fire and ice for long. She got pregnant, and by the time they realized, it was too late. I don't know whether it was decided to break the news to their parents about this development or not, but my father left for his native place."

Parvathi took a deep sigh and moved to the balcony. I followed her.

She looked at me, "The day he left, the results were announced. My father had made it to the IAS, and my poor mother wasn't able to. But she was happy... happy for them, happy for her child." She said in excitement as if living that very moment, but then she fell silent.

"Parvathi?" I probed.

Tears welled up in her eyes and dribbled down her cheeks.

I hugged her intuitively and she started sobbing in my arms.

"He never came back Mohit... he never came back to her."

Then she looked at me with her big black oceanic eyes and said, "You see Mohit, he used her in every possible way – physically, mentally and left her as a used tissue paper."

"But why did he do it?" I said in anger.

"Because suddenly he became crores of rupees worth in dowry. What could a poor Christian family have offered them?"

"Oh!" was all I could say. "Then what happened?"

"My mother heard of his marriage and lost her nerves. Around that time, she was seven months pregnant."

I wiped off her tears with the back of my hand.

"So Mr Mohit, I am an illegitimate child," she said with a sly smile, "born out of sin."

"Your mother did no sin Parvathi," I said with a voice filled with emotion. "To love someone is no sin, and you are a wonderful human being."

"Thank you."

"By the way, did you find out who your father is?"

"Yeah I know, and I can't really do anything about him. He is a senior bureaucrat in the finance ministry now."

I hugged her again. She had gone through a lot in her life and although a little gesture of consolation may not have been enough for the pain she had endured, I felt like hugging her.

I had a newfound respect for her now.

I felt so minuscule in front of her.

My pain was no pain in front of what she had experienced all through her life.

I couldn't even begin to imagine how she would have managed her life and her studies living in an asylum. She was a fighter, a real fighter, and I was inspired to fight back the injustice. She had my back, I knew.

"So, you promise you would join office tomorrow?" Parvathi said detaching herself from me and looking deep into my eyes.

"Yes, I promise," I said.

(III)

The moment I entered office the next day, Chinnan summoned me to his office.

"Where were you?" Chinnan barked in his usual manner.

"I was unwell," I said.

"Huh, and you don't have the courtesy to inform somebody at work... anybody for that matter," he asked raising the pitch of his voice on the last word.

I kept silent. It was usual for him to test the patience of his juniors, especially me.

If I had answered back to him explaining why I was unable to inform the office, it would have angered him more.

He waited for a few seconds, giving me the chance to answer, then continued with his lecture.

Nothing pleased him more in the morning than finding someone whom he could bash and boss around.

It made his day.

"Don't think that the way you are standing here in front of me with a lame look on your face, I will pity you."

He got all worked up, picking up a pen from his desk and pointing it at me.

"Show some sense of responsibility, Mohit, and some sincerity. Always remember, if you would not do the job, somebody else will."

The same applies to you, bugger, I thought, but on the face of it I said, "Sorry Chinnan," just to fuse his temper.

I saw his face expression change, an apology from me pleased his ego.

"It's ok. Remember, this should not happen from the next time," he advised reaching for the back pocket of his trousers.

He extracted a hefty purse from his back pocket and asked, "What's your day plan today?"

"Mmm, I would have to see." I mumbled anticipating that more surprises are to come from him.

"Mr Kapoor from Kapoor and Sons Jewellers called in the morning for the creative brief of their sales advertisement, maybe I would go there."

"No need," Chinnan said pulling out some currency from his purse. "Natasha will take care of it."

Then he passed on a bundle of hundred rupee notes to me. "Here, these are ten thousand, go to my house and hand it over to my wife."

"But I have scheduled a meeting with him this morning," I protested, collecting the bundle of notes from his desk.

"I told you na, Natasha will handle it," he said raising his voice.

"But why? He is my client," I asked in an equally agitated voice.

Chinnan stood up from his seat, fuming.

"Do I have to explain it to you now Mohit? Haan... do I?"

He looked at me with a challenging glare, asserting his superiority.

He thought he would subdue me like he did every time in the past, but enough was enough.

I had endured his behaviour all this while, with a hope that things would get better with time.

I had a hope that I would become old in the system some day and he would stop using me for his household and personal chores, but clearly, I was wrong. The exploitation would never end until I mustered some courage to stand up against it.

"Yes," I said haughtily.

Chinnan looked at me in disbelief.

"What... what did you say? I didn't hear you correctly," he said lending his hands to his ear dramatically.

It was a nice ploy to shake up the confidence of a subordinate. In fact, it would have shaken mine days ago when I had a reason to stay in the agency, because I thought I had some fringe benefits, but those fringe benefits were now gone.

"You heard correctly Chinnan, why should I pass on that client to Natasha?" I said in a calm, controlled, cold voice.

"I will tell you why. I will tell you why," Chinnan repeated in a hissy voice trying to control his temper. He took a round around his desk and walked up to me. His face was contorted with anger and for a moment I thought he would hit me.

He stopped inches away from my face instead and continued with his hissy almost panting voice, "Because, Mr Mohit Chawla," then he waited again as if hyperventilating, "she has been promoted, and from now on, she would be your immediate supervisor... not Yogesh."

He paused for a second, trying to control his breath again, "And you are not here to manage the existing clients, but to develop new ones. So all your existing clients would fall under her purview."

"But I developed those clients," I resisted.

"That year is gone," he waved his hand in a good bye signal and continued bellowing, "They are existing clients now and your duty is to develop new ones." He said all this in a sarcastic mimic tone.

I sensed the pulse knocking my temples. I clenched my fists to control my temper.

It was the day to clear up a few things with him and I was worked up, in full steam.

I looked him in the eyes, chewing every word as I spoke.

"Alright," I inhaled some air to control my breathing, "thank you Chinnan, for reminding me of my duties."

I threw the bundle of notes on the table that were still clenched in my fist

"As you said, my duty is to develop new clients and not to be a private servant to you and your family."

Astonished by the sudden aggression in me, he saw the currency strewn on the floor in amazement for a while.

Then he looked at me and clenched his teeth in anger.

I saw his face distort and turn from red to purple.

I wondered if he was going to have a heart attack.

But he was too shameless to have one. He looked at me with his red eyes and hissed, "Mohit, I hate reactions."

"Even I hate reactions, Chinnan... everybody does. You aren't so special after all."

Having said that, I turned and stormed out of his cubicle.

I heard him shouting. "You stupid fool, your days are numbered in this agency now. I will kick your ass out soon."

I raised my middle finger to the voice coming from behind as I walked off the aisle to the stairs.

I splashed some water on my face. It was necessary to cool down, so I poured some water on my head also.

I looked at my reflection in the mirror of the wash room and saw a haggled tired face with dark circles beneath the eyes.

I sighed. This little war was not over.

I had wrestled with the pig today.

Some wise man has said, the more you wrestle with a pig, the more he would enjoy it and make you dirty.

So, I anticipated more hardships and humiliation coming my way in the days to come.

But I had to buy some time, so that I could find another job.

Having said that, it wasn't hard to find another job, but it was extremely hard to find a suitable one.

Why?

Because people like me, who come from 'have you ever heard of' educational institution of a remote town, were a dime a dozen in Delhi, running errands for various sales companies, courier companies, insurance companies, etc.

I didn't want to be one of them.

I wiped excess water off my hands and thought of Natasha. Soon I would have to face her when I would reach our workstations.

I knew I would never recover from the shock she gave me that fateful evening and now I would have to face another challenge, of her being my reporting supervisor.

I would have to control my recent hatred towards her and my temper because an argument with Chinnan was another thing, he would take his own sweet time in taking revenge from me, but the same cannot be said for Natasha.

She was a liar and a pretty good one at that. She was ambitious, unpredictable, and to say the least, dangerous.

It would be suicidal to confront her upright.

She could blame me for anything – eve teasing, molestation, just about anything and I wouldn't even get a grace period to defend myself.

I would be kicked out of the agency, the very same day.

I have to play along like nothing has happened, I have to act as if I don't know that she ditched me.

I have to act as if I never overheard their conversation.

And that role play would not be so easy.

She was rocking her chair, making faces at her mobile camera when I reached the workstations.

She saw me. I saw her.

She stopped rocking her chair, and a multitude of expressions passed through her face in a flicker.

For an iota of a second I thought she was either shocked or surprised to see me, but then she faked happiness on her face like a skilled actor.

"Heya, back from the vacations?" she said merrily.

"Who said I was on vacation?" I asked in a bland tone.

"You were almost absent for a week," she pretended to be astonished.

"So?" I asked.

"So I thought, you would have gone somewhere" she said in not so pleasing a tone this time, visibly miffed by my attitude.

"I was unwell," I said sitting beside her.

"Oh, what happened?" she said faking concern, immediately changing colour and placed her hand on my arm.

I looked at her hand. Earlier her touch would have smitten me, would have sent electric jolts through my spine, a tingling sensation. Now I felt nothing but disgust.

"Viral," I lied.

"Oh," she slowly removed her hand from my arm.

I looked at her, dejected.

How I could have told her that she was the reason why I was depressed and heartbroken for the last few days.

She was the reason why I had lost interest, why I had lost my hunger, lost my sleep, and my mental peace.

We sat in awkward silence for a while.

Then she spoke again.

"You heard the news?"

"What news? That high profile murder case in town?" I asked pretending she was referring to the headlines in the newspapers that day. Although I knew very well she was talking about her promotion, but I did not want to show any emotion on that account.

She raised her eyebrows and exhaled a lot of air from her mouth, indicating despair and pity.

"Oh dear, poor Mohit, still the same simple man," she said in a pitiful voice and stressed on the 's' of simple as if she had wanted to say silly but settled for simple instead.

"Oh, you meant the recent development in our agency?" I asked, still beating around the bush, still unable to digest that little bit of information.

She looked at the nails of her left hand, observed the filing and the texture of the nail paint, then said, still looking at her hand, "Yes, so? Don't you think you are missing something."

Now I understood what she wanted out of me, that egoist bitch!

"Congratulations Natasha."

"Thank you," she bowed her head just by two degrees in drama. "After so much of hinting and persuasion, it meant a lot to me."

Her tone indicated that she meant just the opposite of what she had said.

We sat in awkward silence for a while, as she checked her mails and I rubbed by hands together in nervousness. I don't know why, but I felt nervous and hopeless at that moment.

She turned from the computer monitor and addressed me in a cold professional tone.

"See Mohit, you and me, we are a team now."

Oh, so we weren't the team earlier, when Yogesh used to be our supervisor, I thought.

"And I don't like to fail."

That I know already.

"We have to excel, by hook or by crook."

Yeah, the same way you did with the 'Employee of the Year' contest, sabotaged my nomination form. I thought and wondered again how she had managed to do that.

"So, I want every little bit of information on what's happening with your clients."

That statement broke my mental monologues.

"Wow Natasha, I think you forgot that we used to discuss everything, almost everything including my clients earlier too." I said sarcastically.

And that is why you managed to betray me, I thought.

"We used to speak on phone for hours, don't you remember?" I added.

"I want a written report on all your clients. ASAP," she responded in a professional tone and completely ditched my onslaught.

You already have that... my client report in the nomination form, I thought but said nothing.

"And we can't be friends like earlier. I am you supervisor now and we would have to maintain a respectable distance," she said in a cold tone.

I looked at her in wonder. I was amazed how people change their attitude overnight.

I was just a subordinate for her now.

How she could forget that we used to roam hand in hand for hours.

But then, how could I forget that it was all a drama staged by her to take advantage of me.

She saw me looking at her.

"What part of ASAP do you not understand, Mohit?"

I sighed and switched on my computer.

(IV)

"Happy birthday to you..., happy birthday to you...dear... happy birthday to you," she crooned in her husky voice. I saw a butler coming towards our table with a small cake on a tray. He placed the cake neatly at the center of the table, bowed and turned around to march towards the kitchen.

It was the chocolate truffle cake, so beautiful.

I choked with emotion looking at it.

For the first time in the day, I felt warmth and love.

I looked at Parvathi with gratitude, she smiled and squeezed my hand in assurance.

She had given me a nice surprise. I had never expected anybody in the office to remember my birthday.

It was not a routine day for me; it was my special day. But there was nobody who could have made me feel special.

Nobody, no family, no old friends, no relatives.

Parvathi had called in the afternoon. She had asked me to pick her up from midway to the office.

I readily agreed, because so far, she was the only friend that I had at the workplace.

So, I met her at Connaught Place, and she said she had some work in Le Meridian hotel and I should accompany her.

I tailed her to the restaurant and then to the table.

"Hey lost boy, will you cut the cake please?" she chided, breaking my chain of thoughts.

I picked up the knife, and looked at her with gratitude, carving a small portion from the cake.

She picked up the piece of cake and rubbed my nose with some chocolate cream before offering me to bite in.

"Thank you Parvathi, for such a nice surprise."

"The pleasure is all mine," she said with genuine warmth in her eyes.

We settled ourselves on the chair for the lunch that she had ordered beforehand.

Most of our lunch went in silence, till the last part when we were having desserts.

"I have some news for you," Parvathi said gulping a spoon full of fresh fruit ice cream.

"What?"

"I don't know how to break it," she said fidgeting with the slice of pineapple in her bowl, "You won't like it."

"Huh, things are way beyond what I like and what I don't," I said in a dejected tone. "So tell me."

"I know what happened to your 'Employee of the Year' nomination form."

That intrigued me. I had always wondered since that party, what the hell had happened. I had after all posted the nomination form to the Director's office. How Natasha got hold of it was still a mystery to me.

"How... how come?" I asked stammering.

"The Director's secretory and I go to the same beauty parlour," she said chewing on the pineapple slice that she was playing with a while ago.

"That I came to know yesterday only when I accidently met her in the beauty parlour."

"Hmm," I uttered, bemused, "so what did she say?"

"I think she is not very fond of Natasha," she opinionated, was toying with the piece of cherry now.

I wasn't really concerned about what the Director's secretary felt about Natasha. I just wanted to know the truth and fast.

"Oho, what did she say?" I said, a bit irritated.

She looked at me displeasingly but continued nonetheless.

"You know how unkempt Director's secretary is. I was surprised to see her in the beauty parlour in the first place."

I nodded in agreement, she was a nerd alright. When I looked at her for the first time, I immediately realized that she had not encountered the breed called beauticians.

Unkempt eyebrows and hair on her arms were her trademark.

But she was very efficient and that's why the Director had chosen her to be the secretary.

She was a bull when it came to work.

It must have been a real special occasion that dragged her to the beauty parlour.

"She screamed like hell, when the beautician waxed her legs." Parvathi continued, "I advised her to visit the parlour regularly, to avoid growth of hair."

I nodded absently in agreement again, as if I was an expert on body hair.

I wondered when she would come to the point.

"You know what she said, Mohit?"

"What?"

"She said that she wasn't like Natasha, beautiful on the outside but mean and a bitch inside. Then she said she knew how that bitch got the 'Employee of the Year' award."

Now my ears were receptive and I was alert and awake, as she had finally come to the point. I took a swig from the glass of water.

"She clearly remembered the day when she received the courier from you. As per the duties defined to her and the procedure, she cut open the courier to determine the importance level of the document, read it and realized that it was the nomination form."

"She took my name?" I asked Parvathi in disbelief.

"Yes, she said that it was the nomination form from Mohit Chawla."

"Then what did she do?" I was on extremities of tension.

"She said that it was simply wrong to send the nomination straight to the Director's office. It had to come from your immediate manager."

Only if you believed in your immediate manager, I thought.

"So, she went to your workstation, to return the nomination form back to you, so that you came via the proper channel."

"But she never came to me," I protested.

"Yes, because you were not there, and Natasha was."

"So?" I asked in a harsh tone, anger rising in me silently.

"That's what I asked her," Parvathi tapped my hand in consolation, reminding me that she was on my side.

"She said that that the bitch sweet talked her to obtain that parcel, assuring that she would hand over the parcel to you. The Director's secretary thought that there was no harm in handing over the parcel to Natasha because after all you two were seeing each other according to the grapevine of the agency."

Yeah I too believed that, that I was steady with her, so how could I blame the Director's secretary now.

I sighed.

Feeling dejected, when the mystery was finally solved, I didn't know if I should be more shocked than hurt.

"So what are you going to do?" Parvathi asked me. "Report the same to the Director?"

"Is she ready to tell the same in front of the Director?"

"I asked her, she said no. She said that she needs this job and does not want to fall into any controversy."

That was expected.

This was another trait of Delhiites, and more so, people working in such agencies, nobody would help you when you need them to stand by.

Otherwise, they would offer plenty when you don't need any.

"Then nobody would believe me," I said wiping my mouth.

Parvathi paid the bill. I checked my mobile phone; there were eight missed calls from the office number and a message. I had my phone on silent since morning and had forgotten to switch it to the ringer mode.

The message was from Sanjay Kumar aka the Owl, our AVP HR. He wanted to see me immediately in his office.

I wondered if there were more surprises in store for me on this day.

We reached the office and I straightaway walked to Sanjay Kumar's office.

He was pacing the corridor when I approached him.

Seeing me, he went to his cabin, signalling me to follow him.

"You want some coffee?" he asked as soon as I settled down on a chair opposite him.

"No, thanks," I said formally.

I looked at his sombre face, and soon had a feeling that all was not well with him.

He extracted an A4 envelope from his desk drawer, took out a printed paper and placed it in front of me.

"What is it?" I asked.

"Read it yourself," he said.

My face flushed red as I started to read the content of the paper.

"Just like that?" I said in a hollow tone after reading the contents completely.

"It's the management's decision."

"But why?"

"See Mohit, the agency is going through a rough patch. There are rumours of recession in the market and advertising gets the first hit."

I swayed my head in denial haughtily; it was more than a mere bad market phase. It was revenge and I knew that.

"Also, we have seen a considerable dip in your productivity. Somehow the management feels that you have lost interest and are not fit for the job," he said in a flat tone.

"What if I refuse to sign on this resignation letter," I said in a fit of rage.

"Then I would have to terminate you."

I stood up from my chair, clenching my fists in anger.

"Then terminate me!"

"Listen to me Mohit. Think with a cool mind and you'll realize that this is the best way. If I terminate you, it would be very hard for you to find another job," he said in a tone that sounded like counselling.

The fat ass had logic behind him. So I dragged the paper towards me and signed it seething with rage.

"Thank you, for this wonderful gift on my birthday." I sneered looking at him and turned to leave his cabin.

"Oh, it's your birthday today. Happy birthday," Sanjay said from behind me.

"No formalities, Sanjay," I said sliding shut the door of his cabin forcefully.

"Hey, it's nothing personal Mohit. Don't think like that," he said in a soft grandfather like tone.

"It is personal, and I know very well who did it," I said seething with rage.

I walked straight out of the agency, picked my bike and raced it to full throttle in fury.

There was no point sticking around in this godforsaken place, in this city.

I failed you this time, mumma, I failed you. I failed in every department. I failed in love and I failed in judging people. This is no place for a true and honest man.

My head wobbled as I drove my bike aimlessly around the city.

I crossed an intersection and jumped a red light at speed clocking to ninety on that old machine.

Somebody honked and screeched behind me, cursing me.

I looked back to see what had happened, never losing the grip on the throttle, never easing the speed of the bike.

Then something hit me, and hit me real hard.

I felt a jolt, a sudden hard jolt. I felt I was in the air for a while, then a crash on something hard, concrete.

Then pain, just acute pain, in the head, neck, back and the complete body, as if a train had hit me head on.

I felt something oozing and dribbling out of my head.

I heard voices, lots of voices.

Then the voices faded slowly and darkness embraced me.

(V)

I love her mom. I have found the meaning of true love. True love is not to find someone whom you love, but to be with someone who loves you.

That somebody is Parvathi, mom. I know she doesn't fit in your image of daughter-in-law.

She is dark, she is not of our caste and she smokes, but she cares for me mumma and that matters the world to me.

I love Parvathi. I love her... and I know she loves me too, but does not realize it yet.

Please mom please, can I marry her?

"Monu, we are with you beta. We all are here, please open your eyes."

I heard the faint voice of my mom. She was there and I wanted to see her, but my eyelids were heavy, very heavy and my body was numb.

I made a final effort to open my eyelids and with droopy eyes, saw my mother hovering over me.

Wearily, I closed my eyes again, but now there was a difference. I could hear her. I could hear mom.

She called for the doctor.

The doctor checked me, I could sense that.

Then I heard the unknown voice of probably the doctor.

"Few hours more Mrs Chawla and he would be completely conscious."

Then I drifted back to sleep for I don't know how many hours.

A commotion at the door woke me up, somebody in a vaguely familiar voice said

"Is he still unconcious?"

"No," I said weakly and opened my eyes, this time with less effort than earlier.

Mom was by my bedside, and I faintly smiled at her.

She gently caressed and kissed my forehead, "Welcome back beta."

"Yessss," I heard an excited voice. "I knew it. He is a tough nut, won't let go easily." Sameer came from behind my mother, grinning end to end.

I saw Satendra Bhandana alias Satty with him, who waved at me.

Then my eyes searched for someone else in the room, someone whom I expected to be there.

But she wasn't there.

"Mom, do you have my mobile?" I asked mom in a tired voice.

"Yes beta, they recovered your mobile from the pavement, but why do you want it now?" she asked.

"Just give it to me Mom."

"But beta, you have just recovered from coma, why do you want your phone now?"

"Oh ho, I want to make a call mom," I said, this time a bit agitated.

"Okay okay," she said in a hurry and rummaged through her handbag, extracted my mobile and gave it to me.

I looked at the mobile in my hand. Its screen was broken and the display was gone. I tried to dial a number but my fingers were numb. I couldn't hold it straight and it fell on the bed.

I looked at the mobile in frustration and then at mom.

"For god's sake Monu, you just got your second life, what's so urgent, who do you want to call?" Mom asked softly but sternly.

"Nobody," I said looking away from her.

"She is here beta, she was right behind you when you spoke. She just ran out of the room," mom said.

"Why?" I asked in confusion.

"Ask yourself," mom said and went out of the room.

I looked around foolishly in the smiling faces of Sameer and Satender.

"Come on beta, don't be shy," I heard mom's voice at the door.

I wondered why Parvathi, the self-proclaimed male basher would feel shy in this set-up, where a patient had just recovered from coma.

Then mom came inside with Parvathi beside her.

Mom was her usual best. She generally is when she is happy, then she would chatter and would talk animatedly for hours.

"You know beta, this girl has not left your bedside since the day she knew you are hospitalized," mom said to me.

"Now when you have gained consciousness, she is shy," she said patting Parvathi's head with affection.

I did not want to question her, because I knew mom would pose a question in order to generate interest and then would answer that herself.

"Because you were blabbering since morning today, Mom, Parvathi is a good girl, she is a good girl and I want to marry her blah blah," she said imitating me.

I smiled at mom's acting, she was really very happy to be doing this jig, and I was happy to see my mom after a long time, although the setting was not much to my liking.

I looked at Parvathi and smiled faintly.

She looked at me with affection, our eyes met and she lowered her gaze.

She was shy alright, because her cheeks had a red tinge, and her eye were moist. I loved the way she looked at me that moment, that look in her eyes said it all. Those black eyes had deep passionate hues in them, with a thousand stories to tell and a million moments to share.

I wondered why I had missed looking so deep in her eyes earlier.

I looked at my mother, she smiled and nodded in affirmative at me, as if approving Parvathi.

But then the mobile which had slipped from my fingers a while ago rang suddenly, ending the perfect moment.

Everybody looked at the sudden intruder with surprise.

I picked up the mobile gently with two fingers of my still intact but bruised hand, and took the call.

It was hard to tell who had called because the mobile set was in a really bad shape.

It was the wonder of wonders why it wasn't in coma, just as I had been.

"Hello," I said faintly in the speaker phone, half anticipating that my kid brother would be on the other side.

"Is this Mr Mohit?" I heard an unknown voice from the other side.

"Yes, speaking," I said, unsure of who could be calling at such a time.

"Mohit, I am M.L. Kapoor from Kapoor Fashions," said the voice at the other end.

"How can I help you sir?"

Sensing my tired voice, mom came forward to grab the phone from me.

I stopped her from doing so and switched the phone to the speaker mode.

"I heard about your work from my friend and I need to do the creatives for my new clothes range," the voice said.

I looked at Parvathi, who was listening to the conversation with rapt attention.

"My friend said, you are good. Can you come and meet me tomorrow?" he asked.

"Hold on sir," I said and pressed the mute button on the phone.

"Parvathi," I grabbed her hand. "Can I ask you something?"

"What?" she said softly.

"Will you be my business partner?"

She nodded yes in response.

"Will you be my life partner?"

Two little tears appeared on the edge of her eyes.

She nodded again in affirmation and turned her head away.

I pressed the unmute button of the mobile.

"Mr Khanna, I am no longer employed with AAA Advertising but I can service you from P & M Advertising Solutions," I said and waited for a reply from the other side.

There was silence on the other side.

I looked at the anxious faces of Mom, Parvathi, Sameer and Satender.

"Hello, any problem Mr Kapoor, are you there?" I prompted the man on the other side.

"Not at all Mohit. I believe people make the companies, and not vice versa."

I smiled in satisfaction and said, "Then I can come next week sir, not tomorrow."

"Why"

"Because I am recovering from a small accident."

"No issues. I can wait. Take rest and meet me next week, bye."

"Bye sir."

The call disconnected.

Mom hugged Parvathi with delight as soon as the call disconnected.

My dear friend Sameer tossed a logical question.

"Congrats buddy for your wife and new life, but tell me, who would give you the start-up money?"

"I would," Satender said raising his hand as if responding to the roll call, even before I started to feel worried about the issue.

I thumbs-upped Satender. He bowed his head dramatically to that.

I closed my eyes in exhaustion but with a small smile on my face.

My head throbbed and I felt drained with so much talking.

But for the first time since landing in the city, I was satisfied and I was happy.

Now that's what I called friends with benefits and work with incentives.

Epilogue

Three years later

I entered the Director's room of my three-bedroom flat cum office and saw her working on the computer.

She was her usual self, earphone plugged in, listening to some music, shuffling in between the story board to Facebook on her computer.

I saw a cube of chocolate stuck in between her fingers. Of late she had left the habit of smoking for good, but was now addicted to dark chocolate.

I silently tip-toed on to her and grabbed her from behind.

She smelled of dark chocolate and her aroma mixed with the smell of the chocolate aroused me.

I kissed her nape passionately.

She wrapped her hands on mine.

"Oh no, what are you doing? I would file a molestation charge on you, boss," she said in a mock shocked voice.

"Please Miss Secretary, don't do that please. I have a wife at home," I said keeping up with her drama, "she would kill me."

"Okay, I will not tell her, but on one condition."

"What?"

"I need a salary hike. After all, I can't juggle myself being a secretary and a creative writer and now I see, you want me also," she said seductively.

I kissed her again, on the cheek this time.

"Mmm, if I would give you the hike, then you would let me do whatever I want?" I said sneaking my hand in her shirt.

One of our five other colleagues sneezed in the main hall.

"Control control, Mr Husband. There are other people in the main hall," she said in a warning tone

"I wondered what would have happened if I had employed a secretary for you," she added, breaking free of my grip.

"Who needs a secretary, when I already have a beautiful one," I said rubbing my nose on her neck stubbornly.

"Huh, I know. All men are the same, including you," she said distancing herself from me.

"Oh, come on Parvathi!" I said in a complaining tone.

She made a face to tease me.

I settled myself on the adjoining table.

"You don't get any news of AAA Advertising, do you?" Parvathi asked, moving her swivel chair in my direction.

"No," I said busily taking out my diary and the power chord of the PC notebook from the table drawer.

Parvathi knew I had no real friends in AAA Advertising but she had spent more years there than me, so sometimes news filtered to her through her acquaintances in the agency.

"Your beloved Natasha got married last Sunday," Parvathi said and looked at me critically as if examining my reaction to the news.

I tried to maintain a poker face.

Internally, my heart gave a sigh. After all, she was my first love.

I was curious to know who in this whole world was so unlucky to be her life partner, and I had a person in mind.

So I couldn't help myself from asking.

"Really, with whom?" I questioned then presented my guess to her, half anticipating it to be true. "Yogesh?"

"Naah, she was too shrewd to be marrying him," she dismissed my guess with the wave of her hand.

"Then?"

"I heard that she was married off to some Singapore-based business tycoon's son," Parvathi moved back to her work, as if the news was hardly important to her, and then added, "Arranged marriage, you know."

That little bit of information left me wondering.

What happened to her ambition?

What happened to her career?

That career, for which she could have done anything, just anything.

That career, for which she became so shameless.

As far as I knew, she wanted to grow on her own, by hook or by crook.

She wanted to show her family that she can stand on her own, but then at last her father's ambition got the better of her ambition.

Ultimately, she had become a business proposition between two business houses.

The desk phone rang on Parvathi's table, she picked it up.

She said hello to someone on the other side and then placed her hand on the speaker phone, and informed me, "Your friend Chinnan is on the line, wants to speak to you."

I looked at her with surprise. Of all the people in the world, Chinnan called me?

I raised my eyebrows enquiringly but she shrugged her shoulders and gave the receiver to me.

"Hi Chinnan, how can I help you?" I said in a business-like tone.

"Hi Mohit, how are you buddy?" I heard his weird tone.

His tone gave me a refresher on what all I had gone through with him as my boss, earlier.

"I am fine, Chinnan, tell me?" I maintained my formal tone.

"See Mohit, Mr Ramakrishnan felt very bad yesterday, that such a talented guy like you left our agency."

"But that was three years ago, Chinnan," I replied coldly.

"Exactly, we felt something was missing, all this long."

"Let's come to the point, shall we?" I wanted to conclude the conversation as soon as possible. "I am not taking your job anymore."

"No no Mohit, you are getting it wrong. We know you are doing well. We want to join hands," Chinnan said in a hurry, fearing that I would disconnect the phone.

"In other words, you want to buy me?" I said in a curt tone.

"Arrey, you are getting it wrong," he said in a pleading tone. "We will make you big."

I judged the immense pressure on him to crack me, by the tone of his voice.

But I had to answer him, once and for all.

"Chinnan, I appreciate that you called me, to buy me out. That means I am doing good, but I am not in the rat race. I never was from the start. I don't want to be big, but I want to do good, however small it is. So tell your Mr Ramakrishnan, that please don't worry, I would not race with him because my ideologies and business ethics are different."

I looked at Parvathi, she gave me a nod.

"Because I can't gel with your ideologies of cheating people, and I don't use unfair means to win clients," I said and quietly place the receiver on the cradle.

I looked at her again. She pounced on me and planted a kiss on my lips.

I was happy, and that's what I always wanted in life. Fringe benefits.

A warm hug and a sweet wet kiss.

Recommended Reading

Wottaplot!
Santosh Vishwanath

Raj sets out to conquer a piece of land around the Bangalore city. Through some humorous and some hopeless misadventures, he realizes that it isn't as easy as it sounded.

While the earlier trigger was to prove a point to someone else, it slowly dawns upon him that he needs to prove things to himself first.

Wottaplot! is the story of an average Bangalorean's plight to own a small piece of land and the adventures that follow.

Santosh makes a living by making sense out of numbers and at the same time, loves to live in a world of words. A true Bangalorean himself, he is fond of telling stories.

ISBN: 9789382665939; Pages: 208; MRP: 195/-; Binding: Paperback

---

Inside the Heart of Hope
Rishabh Puri

Rick has a medical condition that makes his life different from the rest. But he sees this as an opportunity to cherish life and all the bitter-sweet gifts it brings with it.

Amidst frequent visits to the doctor, multiple surgeries that risk his life being, and a life that meant surveillance all the time, Rick falls in love.

Inside the Heart of Hope is a story of strong will, perseverance and optimism which will make you wonder if sky is really the limit.

Rishabh Puri loves to meet new people and explore the world. He enjoys sitcoms and movies, likes to read and experiment in the kitchen.

ISBN: 9789382665960; Pages: 136; MRP: 150/-; Binding: Paperback

Twenty Twenty: A Race Against Time
Anuraag Srivastava

Abhi and Aditi are siblings who want to realise the dreams in the big city. In the midst of all the strugg and success, if they are not able to resolve a crisis i twenty days, their very existence can come und threat. In short, they have to hit sixes on every bounc thrown at them.

Twenty Twenty is a story of betrayal, deceit an relationships, where a master planner devises game to get to his own ambitions.

Anuraag Srivastava has been a banker for over eighteen years now. Present based at Ghaziabad, he is a poet, guitarist, photographer and avid reader.

ISBN: 9789382665915; Pages: 224; MRP: 195/-; Binding: Paperback

---

Messed Up! But All For Love
Arvind Parashar

Neil and Gauri are deeply in love, but Neil's fitne consultant Srinya seems to be stirring some trouble their lives. Drishti is a TV news anchor and journali and her husband Somesh, a top cop. They bump in Neil and his friends in Cuba and things change.

The havoc ensues when Drishti gets abducted ar Neil is framed for it.

In short, their lives are *Messed Up! But All for Love.*

Arvind Parashar has been a corporate leader in firms like GE, Dell ar Genpact. He is a painter who enjoys road trips and gives motivation lectures across leading educational institutes.

ISBN: 9789382665946; Pages: 176; MRP: 175/-; Binding: Paperback